TALES FROM THARASSAS

A THARASSAS CYCLE PREQUEL

J. SCOTT COATSWORTH

Published by
Other Worlds Ink
PO Box 19341, Sacramento, CA 95819

✾ Created with Vellum

I dedicate this book first and foremost to the wonderful community of readers, writers, and publishers who made it possible, chief among these Jim Comer, Ryane Candyce, Kim Fielding, Angel Martinez, Kristin Masters, Jaime Lee Moyer, and everyone else who had a direct or indirect hand in one of these stories.

And as always, I dedicate it to my husband Mark, who has always believed in me and pushed me to do this whole "being a writer" thing, even though it can be a long and lonely road.

Love you all.

FOREWORD

You hold in your hand the prequel to The Tharassas Cycle, which I jokingly call my "four book trilogy."

The three tales in this volume were written at different times over the last few years, and together they provide a backdrop to the events of The Tharassas Cycle that will fill in some of the gaps, enlighten (and hopefully delight) you.

The idea to create this volume came to me about a month before the publication of book one, *The Dragon Eater*, because who needs more than a month to craft a new release? As it happened, I already had two of the three stories written and published, and so it was only a matter of writing the third.

I figured it would be easy! Then I found out how wrong I was. Crafting *The Fallen Angel* was emotionally draining, but in the end, I am really happy with how it turned out.

The stories in this volume are presented in chronological order, not in the order in which they were first written.

The Fallen Angel

The first story in this collection, *The Fallen Angel*, was finished four days before publication, after a mad race through writing, beta reading, rewriting, sensitivity reading, and final proof. It's one of the only stories I have ever written that explicitly deals with race, and this proved to be a huge challenge for me. I want to thank Ryane Candyce for her part in making sure I got the details right (and please attach no blame to her for any that I didn't).

This is the origin story for the *ce'faine*. It tells the tale of Charlie Fah, a young man in what's then called Gully Town, as he deals with the injustices heaped upon him and others who are different - the *differs* - by the mostly white, blond and blue-eyed denizens.

The Last Run

The second story, *The Last Run*, takes place in the same city, now called Gullytown. It was the first story I ever wrote that was set on Tharassas, and is the origin story of the Hencha Queen.

It was inspired by a conversation with Jim Comer, a friend of mine, in which he insisted that FTL (faster-than-light) travel would never be possible. The story explores how an inter-solar civilization might work if all travel between the stars had to max out at just below light speed.

The Last Run was also my first story with two lesbian protagonists, though the main characters' sexuality does not play a large role in the story.

The Emp Test

The Emp Test has a strange, circuitous history. I originally wrote it in the 1990's. It was first titled Autumn Wind, and was the coming out story of a young gay cowboy who broke his leg and spent a couple months recuperating in the care of a young Native American man.

This was long before I became aware of the concept of

"cultural appropriation" - the idea that it's not okay to steal parts of someone else's culture to sell a story, especially if you don't do your homework to get the details right.

And although I sold it in 2014 to a Pacific Northwest journal called Poplorish, I grew increasingly uncomfortable about this fact. Not that there was anything overtly racist about the tale, but it did lean heavily on some stereotypes about Native Americans, and was drawn mostly from my osmotic knowledge of the culture from growing up in Tucson, Arizona.

So when prepared to rerelease the story, I recast it in the Highlands of Tharassas, added some sci-fi pieces and lengthened it considerably. The dynamic between the two protagonists remains the same, but both the culture and details have changed. The emp in this story - a symbiont that plays a key role - was one of the new pieces, and laid the groundwork for much that comes later.

So sit back and enjoy these three tales, and then dive in to the Tharassas Cycle with *The Dragon Eater*.

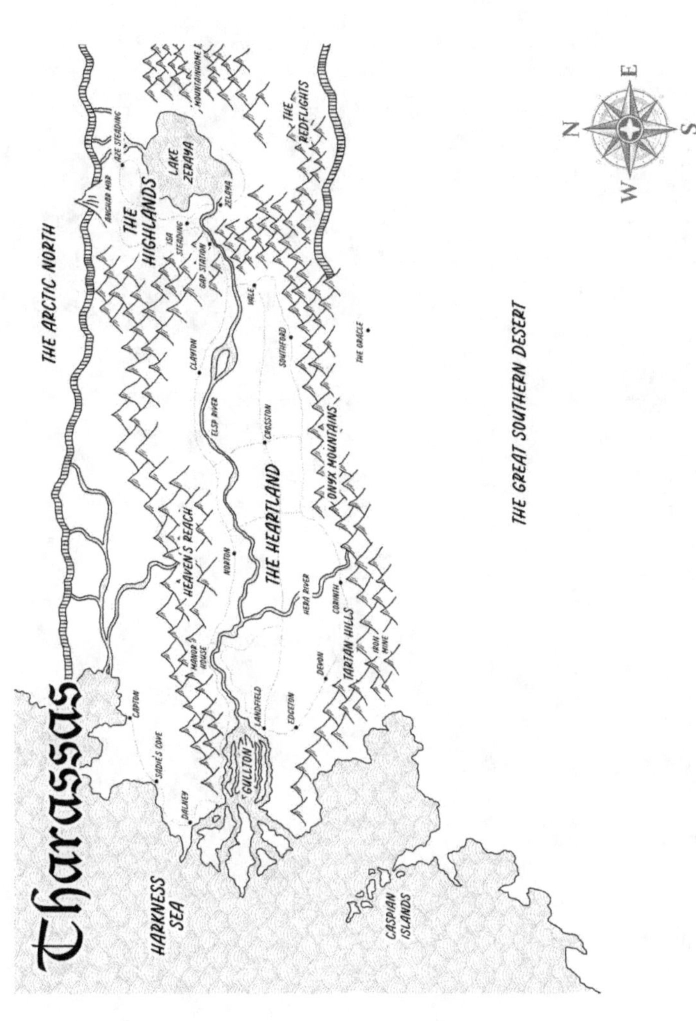

Tharassas
THE ARCTIC NORTH
HARKNESS SEA
THE HIGHLANDS
LAKE ZERAYA
ARCHARD MOR
AXE STEADING
ISA STEADING
GAP STATION
MOUNTAINHOME
ZELOMA
THE REDFLIGHTS
CLAYTON
HALE
SOUTHFORD
THE ORACLE
ELSO RIVER
CROSSTON
CLIFTON
SADIE'S COVE
DALKNEY
HEAVEN'S REACH
HONOR'S HOUSE
NORTON
THE HEARTLAND
GULLTON
LANDFIELD
EDGETON
DEVON
HERA RIVER
ONYX MOUNTAINS
CORINTH
TARTAN HILLS
IRON MINE
CASPIAN ISLANDS
THE GREAT SOUTHERN DESERT
N
E
S
W

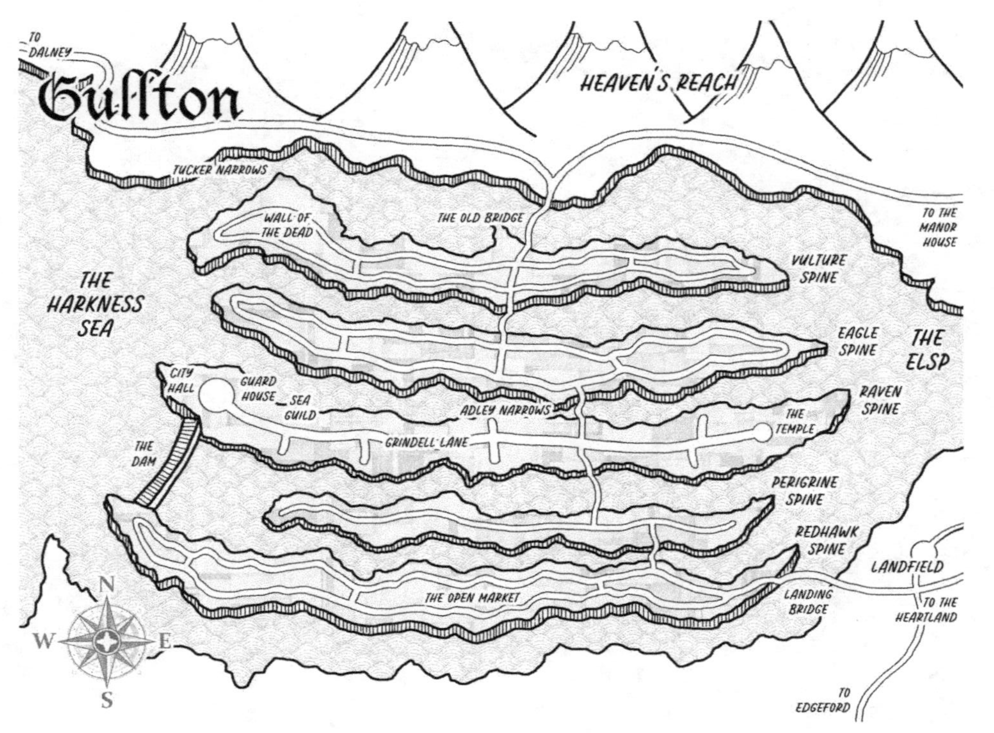
Gullton
TO DALNEY
HEAVEN'S REACH
TUCKER NARROWS
THE OLD BRIDGE
TO THE MANOR HOUSE
WALL OF THE DEAD
VULTURE SPINE
THE HARKNESS SEA
EAGLE SPINE
THE ELSP
CITY HALL
GUARD HOUSE
SEA GUILD
ADLEY NARROWS
RAVEN SPINE
THE TEMPLE
THE DAM
GRINDELL LANE
PERIGRINE SPINE
REDHAWK SPINE
LANDFIELD
THE OPEN MARKET
LANDING BRIDGE
TO THE HEARTLAND
TO EDGEFORD
N E S W

THE FALLEN ANGEL

167 AL, 209 AL

Author's Note: The Fallen Angel takes place on the colony world of Tharassas in the only city called Gully Town. The bulk of the story takes place in 167 AL (after landing), about 250 years before the events of the Tharassas Cycle. The latter parts of this story (the "present day") occur around 209 AL. Gully Town and The Heartland are undergoing a racial reckoning…

DIFFER

"**G**rappa, tell me a story."

I sit back and stare at little Ellya, looking up at me from my lap—all of six years old, and beautiful, her skin the color of the wet earth down by the river. Lighter than mine, but her hair is kinky too, a throwback to one of our ancestors. *Probably an Angel.*

Wind whips the heavy cloth of the tent. Outside, a summer storm lashes the mountain valley where we make our home in the warmer months. Their parents are likely happy for the break from all those inquisitive minds.

Inside it's warm and comfortable, and all the children of the village have gathered here for story time, seated on the woven purple rug that takes up a good part of the tent.

Ioyo, my grandson, sits in the front row, next to his best friend Onley, watching me eagerly.

I kiss Ellya on the forehead, feeling her eagerness through the emp nestled in its pouch on my neck. "What would you like to hear?"

I have many stories from my life of almost seventy years —more than fifty of them spent here in the mountains, taking care of my little flock. In that time, the *ce'faine* have grown to almost five hundred, living a nomadic life spanning three generations. They are my family in the truest sense, my proudest accomplishment.

She reaches up to touch my cheek, her little fingers warm against my skin. "Tell me about the Long Trek."

I close my eyes, a mixture of pain and pride filling me. Such a long time ago, but I still dream about it often, that rough passage that brought us out of Egypt and into the holy land.

I laugh at my own erudition. None of the children here have even the slightest idea what Egypt was. What Earth was.

In our great wisdom, or perhaps our obstinate stubbornness, we decided to make a clean break with the old culture of the Heartland, discarding everything we've been taught and beginning fresh.

I rub my wrinkled chin. "Let's see. It was a very long time ago. You weren't even a wisp in your mother's eye." I look at her—my granddaughter—so perfect in every way. I don't want the world to change her. I don't want her to face the ugliness that I did, growing up in a repressive culture. I want to shelter her from all of that.

Of course, none of us can protect our children from the beauty and peril that life brings.

I stretch out my hands, cracking my old knuckles—a bad habit, that. I take a sip of the herbal tea Merwyn, Ellya's mother, made for me, measuring my time. It's a poor substitute for *akka*, one of my only regrets about leaving the Heartland.

So many years passed. So few left to me. I must teach them while I can, this new generation.

I clear my throat, and the chatter of little voices silences. "Once upon a time, I lived in a wicked place, a cruel city by the sea called Gully Town. There were five islands, like five long fingers—we called them spines. And beyond, only a few small villages and many farms." I close my eyes, remembering that dark time. "They called me Charlie back then. Or Cha'Fah…"

~

"Charlie, come in for supper." Mama's voice emanated from our house down Acton Lane, a small but tidy two room cottage built from flopwood planks. The sun was close to setting in the green sky, but I didn't want to go inside just yet.

"But mama, we're playing *tolus!*"

"Five minutes." Her shadow disappeared back inside. She didn't come outside much—her skin was even darker than mine, and people often laughed when they saw her.

It made my temper boil. I didn't understand why they would do that. She was so beautiful, her lovely hair different from anyone else's on the street. I didn't understand how the world worked then.

"Why do you look like that?" Tom'Mer—we called him Tommer—was a latecomer to our little group of friends. His parents had moved to Gully Town from one of the newer settlements along the southern rim of the great valley of the Heartland—I couldn't remember the name of it. Cornish? Corrint?

"Like what?" I looked like I always had.

"Why is your skin so dark?" I hated Tommer. Before he arrived, no one in my group of friends had ever made fun of me. *Not like that.*

I didn't let his question bother me, much. I'd answered it too many times before. "Why is your skin so light?"

Juli laughed. She usually took my side. "He's right. You look like you live in a cave."

Tommer growled, and all the other kids laughed at him. "Mom says you and your family are dirty. That your kind shouldn't live here."

That was it. I threw myself at him, knocking him to the ground, punching him in the ribs.

He grabbed me and rolled us over, and started pummeling me back, his face twisting in red rage. "You stupid dirty *differ!*"

I snarled and pushed him off. We separated, getting to our feet and staring warily at one another, like a couple caged *eircats*.

Our friends encircled us, looking unsure. We'd never had a real fight in our group.

I didn't care. It was bad enough that he was insulting me, but to go after my family? "I may be *different,* but *you're* the dirty one," I shot back, feeling reckless. "I saw that *aur stye* you call home. How does it feel to live in your own filth?"

"Take it back." Tommer pushed me, knocking me back to the ground.

I hit my head in one of the cobblestones and yelped.

"Leave him alone." Juli put herself between Tommer and me, her hands balled into fists on her hips.

"What's it to you?" Tommer still sounded belligerent, but also unsure what to do. Probably didn't want to hit a girl.

I scrambled to my feet and pushed past her, slamming into him hard and pushing him back into Mim Asha's house and knocking the wind out of him.

He sank to the ground, gasping for breath.

"Don't you ever talk about my family like that again." I was shaking all over.

Then my mother was there, towering over us, a scowl on her face. "You all right, Charlie?"

I hated when she used my full name in front of my friends. "I bumped my head, but I'm fine."

She nodded. "Go home. I have something I need to take care of." She grabbed Tommer's arm and hauled him up. "Your mother and I are going to have a little talk."

I watched them go, full of anger and embarrassment and a sense of familial pride.

Juli touched my shoulder. "You okay, Charlie?"

I reached out to touch the back of my head. It was wet with blood. "I... think so. Just a cut." I looked over my shoulder at our little house, tucked in the long row of small houses. "I gotta go."

She squeezed my hand. "See you tomorrow."

I went home, unhappy with the day, wishing mama would come back. The word *differ* spun around in my head.

In a few moments, she did, closing the door tightly behind her and leaning against it as if she meant to hold it closed against an invading army. "Well, that's that." She sat me on a stool next to the counter where she prepared our meals and checked the back of my head.

"Is it... bad?" I imagined gushes of blood, running down my neck.

Mama shook her head. "Just a little gash." She took a clean cloth and some soap and a little warm water from the hearth. "This is going to sting, but we best get that cleaned up. You're gonna have a good bruise around your left eye, though."

I stiffened as she dabbed away the blood, but it wasn't so bad. Mama's touch calmed me.

Our house wasn't fancy like Juli's—five rooms on two stories—but mama kept it meticulously clean, often with my unwilling help. Much cleaner than Tommer's.

Papa came home early, for once. He often pulled the late shift at the tanner's shop, taking the hours no one else wanted. I didn't know it then, but he was treated badly for having married a woman that most of his friends found unsuitable.

Unsuitable. A word that disguised a multitude of ugly thoughts.

"What's the little scamp done now?" Papa peeled off his

jacket, hanging it to air out on the clothes rack on one of the side walls of our main room.

I bobbed my head, embarrassed. I *hated* disappointing my father.

Mama squeezed my shoulder. "Just a little trouble with some of the neighborhood kids. Nothing he couldn't handle."

I looked up my mother gratefully.

"Looks like you're going to have a shiner there." He hugged me, and the stink of the day fell away. "Proud of you, son."

My chest swelled.

Mama handed me a bowl of soup, filled with hearty vegetables and what looked like aur meat—a special treat. We really had meat in our household. She must've traded one of the other mothers for it.

There wasn't much, so I savored it, biting it into little pieces and chewing on them contentedly to extract all the rich flavor.

When she tucked me into bed later that night in the smaller second room we shared for sleeping, she knelt beside my ear and whispered. "Life is always going to be different for us, my little one. It's something your father will never understand, though gods bless him, he tries."

I thought about it. "I don't *want* to be different." I remembered how Tommer had looked at me and shuddered.

Differ.

My other friends had never treated me that way, but they seemed to follow his lead all too easily.

"I know. But you stood up for yourself today." She kissed me on the forehead, gently brushing my bruised cheek with her warm, lithe fingers. "I'm sorry you had to see how ugly the world can be, but I am proud of you, Cha'Fah. Tomorrow will be a better day."

Her use of my formal name made me feel all grown up. "Promise?" I stared into her kind brown eyes.

"Promise." She pulled the covers of the hand-knitted blanket over me and touched my cheek again with her warm hand. "Sleep tight, Charlie."

My mother was right about many things, but she was wrong about that.

The next day was worse.

ANGEL

Years later, when I was almost an adult, a difficult time descended on Gully Town.

Every year in late winter, the storms descended upon the spines for a full month, filling the valley of the Heartland and dusting the mighty slopes of Heaven's Reach with snow, making the air as thick as soup.

Then when I was seventeen, the rains didn't come.

At first, no one was too worried. Water still flowed down the Elsp, diverted into fields to grow our crops. The Heartland was fairly comfortable year-round, not like our mountain home now, where the winters will freeze your toes off. And we had gotten comfortable there, too.

But as the weeks passed into months and the weather remained dry, people started to worry. And they did what they always did when they were afraid—looked for someone to blame.

My old nemesis Tommer had moved away, but his slur didn't leave with him. Most of the neighborhood kids had taken to calling me *differ*.

I'd broken a few noses over it, and that shut them up, mostly.

There were others like me, or rather, unlike them—scattered around Gullton—skin a dozen different hues, hair that was red or brown or black, eyes that weren't "gully town blue." I'd see them on the street, and we'd nod, bonded by our difference.

Then into the midst of the dry kindling of the drought, a Run from Earth arrived. The news spreading ahead of it like wildfire.

At first, it was hailed as *salvation*. The Angels would save us. Some said they would bring a miracle technology that would feed a hungry world. Others claimed there would be seeds that would grow without water.

People will say the stupidest things when they're scared. But they needed *something* to believe in, and the approaching cargo ship from Earth supplied what they required most —hope.

I'd taken to staying home with my mother during those harsh times, only venturing out occasionally for my weekly school lessons, or to get something from the Open Market. I shaved my head and went out at night, often wearing a hood, when it was easier to pass for a "normal" Gullander.

Nevertheless, I decided to go see the Landing.

It was an event, a grand festival—something that happened only a couple times in a lifetime. Earth was an impossible distance away, farther than you could ride an aur in a thousand years. *Maybe a million.*

So I put on my finest clothes—a newer, pressed ochre tunic and pair of breeches that mama had made for me the year before, bleached a bright white that looked beautiful against the rich tones of my skin, and finished it off with a pair of boots my father had made for me himself, dyed to match my shirt.

The crowd gathered at the edge of the landing field, behind the stone markers, and watched the ship descend. The grasses there were dry... the council had ordered a twenty-foot fire break be cut along the far side, where the huge open patch of land backed up against the farmlands and the hencha field, just in case.

Half the town must have been there, surging across Landing Bridge in waves to gawk at the new arrivals. People were laughing and pointing at the empty sky, each gully bird or cloud spotted starting a new round of excitement. They drank hencha wine served by vendors who had popped up along the roadway that bordered the field and chattered excitedly about the coming event.

I kept to myself as much as possible in the crowd, but I was buffeted by others and given dirty looks when they noticed that I was different. There were a few others like me there—most had wisely decided to stay home—but I was determined to witness the rare miracle with my own eyes.

You've never been to Gully Town, but the populace there is overwhelmingly *white*. They came here to escape the "oppression" of Old Earth, foisting its *diversity* on them and forcing them to *conform*.

People like us were born into their world, and we only lived there with their forbearance. The crowd awaiting the landing was Gullton norm, and those like me who weren't stood out like sore thumbs.

A stranger bumped into me and growled something that chilled me to the bone. "Go home, you dirty *differ*." The voice's owner was an old woman, her hair long faded from blond to a scraggly gray, plastered to her wrinkled forehead by sweat. The look on her face was venomous, as if she'd just glimpsed the man who'd killed her first-born son.

"Sorry." I hated myself for apologizing. Confused, I backed away, taking refuge in the crowd. *How did she know that word?*

"It's coming!" Someone pointed at the sky and a thrill went through the crowd.

For a moment, I let myself forget about the incident, about the unexpected slur.

I looked up in wonder, staring at the tiny lick of flame. For a moment, I was just like everyone else, caught up in the excitement as we awaited our salvation.

The ship grew rapidly from the size of a pebble to a giant boulder that plummeted out of the sky toward us. It was both scary and awe inspiring, the idea that people like us—like me—could build something like that, a carriage to cross the vast gulf between stars.

It wasn't at all what I expected, something sleek and silver. Instead it was blocky, like someone had stuck a bunch of pricks together. It was silver-ish, though the surface was pitted and scarred.

With one last roaring burst of flame that threatened to deafen us all, it settled slowly to the ground, shaking the earth beneath my feet, somehow miraculously not starting a fire. It came to rest, and a sudden, shocking silence settled across the land.

The crowd was still for one long, quiet moment, the only sound the lonely lowing of the wind through the dry grass.

Then a great cheer went up, and we all surged forward.

It was *run or be trampled*, so I ran with the rest of them. I was young and strong and healthy—not the wasted shell of a man you see before you today—and so I was near the front when the ship's hatch opened.

The crowd stopped, uncertain, as a panel opened and a wide ramp descended to the ground. I squinted, trying to make out what was inside, behind that bright light. I didn't have to wait long.

Three Angels descended from on high, like in the Old Faith. I said a prayer to *El'Oss*, crossing my chest in the symbol for infinity, blending both faiths as a *just in case*.

They wore full body suits and helmets, as if they were unsure if our air was safe to breathe, and I swear they shone with their own light, though maybe it was just the refraction from the sun behind them.

Then, one by one, they lifted them off.

The first Angel could have been straight out of the Gully Town theater. She was tall and blond and beautiful, with perfectly symmetrical features and piercing ice-blue eyes.

I didn't realize how conditioned I was by my oppressors until that moment. She was beautiful to me too, but it was an alien beauty, an ideal people like me would never achieve.

The second was also white as an inthym, though he would lose points in the eyes of the locals for his dark hair. Still, he was handsome enough, if you overlooked his blocky nose.

Then the last one removed his helmet.

I stared at him, literally stunned into silence.

He was *magnificent*. I still say that word today when I think about him. Mama had talked about Angels like him, but to see it with my own eyes…

His skin was as dark as the night sky, and his smile radiant when his eyes met mine. His hair was short and curly, like my own when I let it grow out. And he was tall—taller than the others by at least ten centimeters.

And he looked like me.

A hiss went through the crowd, and that word passed around me like a vile, poisonous fog.

Diff diff differ …

I felt the blood drain from my face. For once, I think I was as white as those pale faces all around me.

The Angel must have felt it too. His smile slipped away, and he looked out at the twisted faces all around me uncertainly.

The goddess raised her voice. "People of Tharassas, my name is Captain Jena Stark. We have brought you much-needed supplies. Who is the responsible authority here?"

Our leader stepped forward, bowing obsequiously,

though he cast a suspicious glance at the Angel. "I am Meer Ecton, and I welcome you to our humble village."

"We're glad to make your acquaintance, Meer. I look forward to a profitable and fruitful trade.

The mood shifted again, and a cheer went up from the crowd.

The Meer held up his skinny old arms and played to his audience. "We're in the midst of a difficult drought, and you bring us hope."

The cheer grew louder.

I met the gaze of the Angel once more and shrugged, trying to express so many things in one gesture.

How amazing it was to see someone like me in the garb of an Angel.

How sorry I was that he had come here.

How much I wished things were different.

Then I backed away into the crowd and away from his sight. I pushed my way to the back and burst out of the cheering knot of people, all but running back toward Landing Bridge and the streets of Gully Town.

The city was all but deserted that afternoon, with everyone across the river at the grand event. I did see Mim Kelley sweeping out her chandler's shop. She waved and smiled at me as I passed. She had always been kind.

When I got home, mama smiled at me. She was doing laundry for the neighborhood, making a few extra croners for the household. "How was the Landing?" She stared at the ceiling wistfully. "I went to one when I was about your age, and I still think about it sometimes." Whether those memories were good or bad, she didn't say.

I hated that she had to clean the shit stains of those entitled bastards who ran this town. "It was… interesting." The chant went through my head again. *Diff diff differ…* "There was an Angel there… an Angel like us."

Our eyes met, and hers widened. She set down the fine

woolen short she'd been folding to give me her full attention. "Tell me."

Her grandfather had been an Angel, but this one was far too young to be him. I was sure of that much. Of course, there were many things I didn't know, or thought I knew and was wrong about. When you're young, you think you know *everything*.

"His skin was the most beautiful color, dark as night, and his hair—it was curly, like mine. And when he smiled..." I struggled to identify the feeling that surged in my breast. *Pride*. "He made me feel proud." Mama had once told me your skin got darker when you did good things. He must have been very good. Or so I wanted to believe.

Mama's eyes were wet. She pulled me close, hugging me so tightly that I couldn't breathe. "I love you, little one."

I stiffened. "Mama..." I managed, and she loosened her grip, but only a little, holding me like that for what seemed like an hour.

"Mama, enough." I squirmed out of her grasp at last, smoothing out the wrinkles on my shirt.

She smiled wanly, a sadness in her that I didn't understand, then.

I plowed ahead, heedless of her quiet pain. "So it was all right." My sense of awe had passed, replaced by a creeping worry. I'd seen the ugly mood of the crowd, and hoped they wouldn't hurt him.

Then again, he was an Angel. I supposed he could protect himself. I supposed, too, that I would never see him again.

As it would turn out, I was wrong on both counts.

I got out the precious pad of paper and charcoal mama had bought me for my seventeenth birthday, and began to draw, tracing his tall, proud lines from memory so I would never forget what he looked like. As I drew, she worked on her laundry, and we settled into a companionable silence together.

When it was done, I showed him to her.

I was surprised when she burst into tears.

I wouldn't know why until later.

BACK IN THOSE DAYS, I would fall asleep easily as soon as my head hit the grass-stuffed pillow. But for the last few nights— ever since I'd seen *him*—I had tossed and turned, remembering that proud, kindly face, those eyes, that smile. So like my own.

I'd even thought about going to the landing field again, where a furious few days of trading were in progress. Crafters and artisans, vintners, and half the guild masters and journeymen in Gully Town were lining up with their wares, hoping to snag a bolt of cloth or a set of silver utensils or something else they could brag about to their neighbors: "It's from Earth."

Translation, "No one else has anything like it."

For a time, everyone seemed to have forgotten about the drought, although there were mutterings in town about the lack of a miracle from the so-called Angels. Sure, there were some new corn seeds that were supposed to double the harvest, and some spare parts to repair the Heartland's aging fleet of flitters. There were even a couple new craft, shiny as if they'd just come out of their factory on Earth, for all that they were now twenty-five years old.

But nothing that would turn around our dire situation. Ugly rumors started to circulate:

That the Angel had brought down bad luck upon us.

That Earth was going to cut us off.

That they'd only sent trinkets, despite knowing how bad things were on Tharassas. Which was aur shit, because the ship had launched a quarter of a century earlier, long before our current drought.

But rumors don't feed on sense and logic, and they found a fertile soil that spring in Gully Town.

That's when there was a knock on our door, late at night, after we'd all gone to bed.

I wasn't sleeping well again, lost in thoughts about my Angel. When I first heard the tapping, I thought I was imagining it, but when it sounded again, I peeled back the covers and slipped off of the mattress, my feet cold on the bare wooden floor. I cocked my head, and there it was again—a knock at our door.

Mother and father were fast asleep, curled in each other's arms on their own bed at the far side of the small room. I stared at them, uncertain if I should wake them, and then took a deep breath and headed out of our shared bedroom and through the main room of the cottage to the front door. With the shutters latched, it was dark inside the small space at night, but I knew my way through it like I knew the back of my hand.

I reached to unlatch the door, and then stopped, gripped by a sudden uncertainty. What if it was someone here to rob us? What if it was a functionary from the city, come to harass us over some small infraction?

I snorted. That was a ridiculous idea. No city official would come here in the middle of the night, wasting an opportunity for sleep.

The whole *robbery* idea wasn't so beyond the pale, though, but I was young and strong. I slipped back to the kitchen corner and retrieved mother's paring knife, just in case.

Shivering in the cold, I opened the door wearing just my sleeping clothes.

A man was standing there, taller than me. He was dressed just like us, in the loose fitting homeweave clothing of a peasant. But when I looked up to his face, I saw he wasn't like us at all.

He was like *me*.

The Angel smiled and winked at me. "May I come in? It's colder than winter in New York City out here."

My jaw dropped open as I stared at him. I had no idea what *New York City* was, or why it would be so cold, and I must've looked like an idiot. "You're… the Angel."

He nodded and thrust out his hand at me. "Joliver Eckston. Nice to meet you." He shivered. "But seriously, may I come in? It's colder than a witch's tit in this town."

I had no idea what a witch's tit was either, but I got the picture. I was still in shock. He was *here*. "Forgive me. Come in."

The Angel ducked under the door frame and entered our house. Looking around, I was embarrassed for the rudeness of our living quarters. This man had traveled the stars to reach us, and he deserved someone better. Something better.

"Charlie, what are you doing…" My mama had appeared from the bedroom, and she squeaked when she saw the tall man standing there. Then her eyes went wide, and she reached out to touch him, stopping an inch from his face. Her eyes narrowed. "You look just like Charlie."

"What's going on?" My papa this time, emerging from the bedroom, somehow fully dressed. "Who in the holy green hell are you? And what are you doing in my house in the middle of the night?"

I threw myself between them, spreading my arms to protect the newcomer from papa's wrath. "It's all right. He's an Angel."

My mother spoke at the same time. "His name is Joliver."

Both Joliver and I turned to stare at her. How could she know? He'd only just introduced himself to me.

Joliver's mouth worked, but nothing came out for a few seconds. At last he managed to speak. "You look so much like her." Something like rapture crossed his face.

Papa growled. "With somebody please tell me what's going on?"

"Everyone, please sit." Mama was flushed—the first time I ever remember seeing my mother blush. "I'm sorry we don't have any proper chairs. Charlie, get an extra cushion out. I'll put on a cup of hot akka, and we can all talk about this."

We occasionally had company, and so we kept a couple extra stout pillows in the back of the bedroom.

Joliver and my father circled each other warily, taking seats across the low table from one another, two *eircats* sizing each other up before a fight.

I went back to the bedroom to grab the cushion. I placed it at the table between them and sat down, hoping to be a buffer between the two men.

I stared at my father, seeing him with the eyes of an almost-adult. He looked old, far more so than he had the day before, the creases on his forehead deepened to almost-cracks, his skin turning translucent and rough. It was strange to think of him that way—he had always been my pillar of strength, the one I could run to when I just needed something solid in this world to hold onto and to believe in.

Joliver looked so much younger. If I was right about who he was…

My mother slammed down four mismatched mugs full of akka—she had prepared them in record time. The rich aroma infiltrated my nostrils and supercharged my senses.

My father took a long sip of his, closing his eyes, a wide smile crossing his lips. "This is why I married you." When he opened them, he seemed calmer, but his gaze shifted immediately back to our visitor. "So who are you, and why are you here in the middle of the night?"

Joliver took a long sip before answering. "My name, as I've just told my new friend here, is Joliver Eckston. As you can probably tell by the color of my skin, I'm not from around here."

That got a rueful chuckle from my father, which quickly

subsided, the frown returning. "You're an Angel. So how do you know my wife?" There was a dangerous edge to that question that only someone who knew my father well would've heard.

When he got angry, he also became more controlled, channeling that anger into an intense focus that scared even me. My father was an *eircat,* and he would protect his den with the same ferocity when threatened.

My mother slammed her mug on the wooden table, shattering the tension. "Enough of that. We have a guest." She took my father's hand and squeezed it. "Joliver, this is my husband, Max'Fah. Or Maximillian to his close friends. You've already met my son Charlie."

She took a deep breath and sighed. Then she picked up the cup and downed it in one quick gulp. I got a whiff of hencha wine as she set it down again.

"Charlie, Max, Joliver here is my father."

We all turned to stare at Joliver.

His hands gripped the edge of the table, and then relaxed, and for some reason he looked right at me when he replied. "When we travel between the stars, it's a very long journey. It takes twenty-five years, give or take, to reach here from Earth, and the same to go back."

I knew that—it was something they taught us in school, in our weekly sessions. It was hard to imagine how far away from Tharassas Earth actually was.

Joliver continued. "It would be really boring spending the entire trip just staring at the stars. So we… sleep, most of the time."

My father nodded. "But even asleep, you would age…"

"It's not that kind of sleep. We close our eyes and go into a kind of hibernation—a deep freeze. When we wake up, it's as if almost no time has passed."

I stared at him, my mouth agape again. He really was an Angel. To have the power to never age… Still, something was off. I was quite smart too, back then. "If you were here fifty years ago…"

Joliver nodded. "Your grandmother was an older woman. She was quite beautiful, and strong willed, not afraid to go against the wishes of her parents. We only spent a brief time together… a week out of a lifetime. I can still see her. It was just a couple months ago, for me." He closed his eyes. There was a sad longing in his voice that broke my heart. "I took the next run back…"

Mother sighed, her hand on her chest. She'd always had a soft heart for romance. "Mama used to talk about it. She never got over you, you know."

Mama kept a small painted portrait of gramma by her bed —she'd been as white as papa.

Joliver bit his lip. "It wasn't supposed to be like that. I… wanted to stay. But my captain made me leave with the crew." I saw the regret carved in the lines of his face. "Adria was so different from the others. Not judgmental. Not looking at me funny because I looked so different than the… Gulltonites?"

"Gullanders." I stared at him, trying to understand. "It's not like this… back on Earth?" My teachers had always been cagey about that.

Joliver laughed. "No, it's nothing like this. Not anymore. There are people there of all kinds—even more than there used to be. People with antennae, one even with wings, though I don't know if he could really fly."

"Wings?" I tried to imagine it.

"Like a raven." He grinned again.

I had no idea what a *raven* was—well, there was Raven Spine, one of the five long, narrow islands of Gullton—but I was starting to like this Joliver black giant and his strange Earth sense of humor.

Mother narrowed her eyes and cocked her head. "So how did you find us?"

"I saw Charlie here at the landing. I knew immediately who he must be, if not his name." He picked up his cup and took a thoughtful sip. "This was her house too. I came here hoping… I don't suppose she's still alive?" He asked it casually, but his wrist trembled.

My mother reached across the table and put her hand on his. "No, I'm so sorry. She passed away a couple years ago, after a long bout with heartland fever."

Joliver inhaled sharply and closed his eyes.

My heart broke for him. He'd had spent half a century planning to return here to see my grandmother, only to find out that he'd missed her by a handful of years.

The universe is a far stranger place than we know.

He must've felt my eyes on him, because he gave me a wan smile. "Don't feel sorry for me, Charlie. It was a beautiful flame, an affair that lasted a matter of days. For me at least. And how lucky am I, that I get to come back and meet my daughter and my grandson, grown into such beautiful people as the two of you?"

Mama beamed at that, and even papa's sharp look softened a bit.

I had so many questions. *What was Earth like? How did you become a space pilot? How did you meet my grandmother? Why did you come to see us… was it only to try to find her?*

And the most important of all. *Would you take me back with you?*

I didn't belong here. I'd felt it for as long as I'd been able to think, and feel. This world didn't want people like me—it was clear every time I stepped outside.

But before I could ask any of them, we were interrupted by a harsh banging on the door. "Max, you in there?"

I knew that voice. It was Sam'Ost, one of our neighbors. Whenever they came around, our neighbors always asked for my father, never my mother.

"Excuse me. I'll send him away." My father got up and padded to the door, opening it just a crack.

"Sorry to bother you, Max, but Mim'Ost, she said she seen something right strange, a few minutes back."

My father kept the door mostly closed, so I couldn't actually see Sam's face, but I could in my mind. He was a big man, his florid skin ruddy from the fires of his forge, and he always had an angry look about him, as if the world owed him something and he was going to make it pay.

"Ask him about the Angel!" There was a grumbling of other voices in the background.

He's not alone. I looked at my mother in alarm.

"Stay calm. Your father will deal with this." But I heard the quaver in her voice. She looked at Joliver, and he nodded, calm as a frozen pond.

"You all need to go back home. It's late and I want to get back to sleep." My father's voice was strong and deep, normally enough to dissuade others from taking actions they might regret later. It had worked with me on many occasions.

This time, though, it didn't.

"Let us see the Angel, and then we'll go." There was a dangerous edge to Sam's voice, too.

Not for the first time, I wished there was a back way out of our home.

"Good night, Sam. We can talk about this in the morning." Papa tried to close the door, but it was shoved roughly open, slamming him against the wall.

I shrank back out of instinct, and then leapt up, ready to defend my father. I was tall too, but I was no match for Sam's bulk.

He swaggered into the room as if it were his own, looking around until his eyes came to rest on Joliver. Behind him, several of his henchmen filed into the small space, filling it to almost-bursting.

The Angel was on his feet too next to me, glaring at the intruders.

"There he is, boys." He sneered, looking comically evil, but somehow that didn't help the fear I was feeling.

"Get. Out. Of. My. House." The words ground their way out of my throat, fueled by the hatred I felt at that moment for the man who had violated our home. Behind me, I could feel my mother's pride, burning off her like sunshine.

Sam sized me up. "You've grown into quite the man, Charlie." He signaled with his thumb. "Now get out of our way."

I swung at him, but he caught my hand in his fist as easily as a fisherman catches a *kerint*, and forced me slowly down to the ground. I blushed angrily, trying to fight him, but he was far stronger than me.

My father had recovered. He threw his arms around our neighbor's neck and squeezed.

Sam choked and let me go. I fell to the ground and shook my hand—it ached. I hoped he hadn't broken any bones.

Sam threw my father off as if he were nothing, slamming him into the wall a second time. He slid to the ground, gasping for air.

Static energy filled air, raising the hairs on my arms.

I looked around for the source.

Joliver's arms were wrapped in coruscating white sparks of energy. "Get back," he hissed.

I scrambled behind him as he slammed his hands into Sam.

The man practically flew out the open door, knocking over a couple of his friends in the process.

Papa caught his breath and stood unsteadily. "Thank you, Joliver." As if people did that sort of thing all the time. Papa's eyes met mine. "Help me take this trash out."

He lifted one of the remaining men by his arms, and I grabbed his legs. Together we threw the man out onto the street. We did the same with the other, and papa slammed and locked the door behind them.

There was something laying on the floor where one of the men had been. Curious, I picked it up. It was a long loop of rope, tied into a noose, the sort they used to hang murderers and child molesters in the town square, if they didn't burn them on a pyre in Landing Field.

I shuddered, and held it up to show the others.

Joliver's eyes went wide for reasons I still don't understand, beyond the sheer fear and anger it must have inspired in him.

Then he pulled me to his chest and held me tight. "I am so proud of you, Charlie. My grandson."

It should've been strange, this man I barely knew who wasn't much older than I, calling me grandson. But somehow, it was exactly what I needed.

"You should go while they're disorganized." My mother sounded distressed, and she pulled on the bottom of her apron the way she did when something deep and concerning was on her mind.

Joliver nodded. "Will it be safe for you here?"

She touched papa's arm for support. "I… I don't know."

I stared at her, slack-jawed yet again. *How could she not know?* All my life, she'd made this a safe place for me. For us. To see her this way…

A rage built in me, an anger at these intruders who had exposed my parents for who they really were—*human*. I began to form a plan of action, something that had been in the back of my mind for a long time.

Joliver seemed to come to a decision too, nodding sharply. "I'll lead them off. I have a few more tricks up my sleeve." He winked at me. "It was a great pleasure to meet you, Charlie Fah. Your grandmother would be quite proud of you."

I blinked, unsure how to feel about that. "Thank you."

He shook my father's hand. "Take care of them." He

glanced at mama and me again, his eyes growing wet. "They're more precious than you know." Then he unlocked the door and slipped out.

I heard howling outside, not unlike that of a wild animal. It quickly faded into the distance as he drew the angry mob away.

Five minutes later, we had packed up everything important, and slipped out the door, bound for my Aunt Millie's house on Eagle Spine, where we hoped we would be safe for the night.

~

I BLINK. While I've been telling my story, the sun has set, and it's starting to get dark in the camp. The storm has passed on into the mountains, and the air smells fresh and clean.

Ellya touches my face, so like her great-grandmother that it startles me, bringing me back to the present. "Why did they treat you differently?"

I close my eyes and think about the answer. "People learn to hate things that are different." It's a hard truth. Honestly I'm not sure she was ready for it, but I learned it when I was her age, from hard experience. I say a prayer of thanks to the mountains that she only has to learn about it second-hand.

"I thought different was good?" She looks up at me, her face serious.

"It is." It was the foundation of being chefaine—accepting that everyone's differences were a source of great strength—and something we instilled in our children from birth. "But not everyone is as smart as you." *Or as kind.*

Ioyo, her older brother, stares at me from his place on the thick woven rug, his eyes narrowing. "That's stupid."

I chuckle. "You're right. It *is* stupid. But when you live as long as I have, you realize how stupid some people can be." I smile. "Even your own parents."

Ioyo's eyes go wide at that.

I laugh again. I forget how much these children idolize their parents.

They're not wrong. Merwyn and Allyn are good people, raised without the prejudices I grew up surrounded by. We've lived a charmed life here in the Highlands, far away from the Heartland and her poisons, but one day we will have to reckon with them and find a new path forward. "I used to think my own parents were perfect. Don't get me wrong, they were wonderful people. But they were as trapped in their time as we are in ours."

I reach out to tousle Ioyo's hair. He is young and strong, beautiful, a warrior at heart. He will chase *ix* across mountain slopes and maybe even fight *eircats*, one day. I wink at him, and he grins.

I ease Ellya off of my lap and clap my hands. "Off with all of you. Your parents will be waiting for you. We'll finish the story tomorrow."

"Awwww." There's a general sigh of sadness, but that dissipates as they scamper out of the tent to get dinner. The cool air sweeps in, reminding me that it's going to be a chilly night.

I get up from my chair and stretch my old bones. I'm an old man now, long past my prime. My hair has thinned and mostly fallen out, and my skin has wrinkled with age. My joints ache most of the time, and my bones creak sometimes when I stand, which is increasingly difficult during the long, cold mountain winters. But inside I still feel young.

Age is a funny thing. The older you get, the more you need to sit, and the more your body punishes you for doing it. I miss the spry young man I once was, even if I don't miss the circumstances of that time.

I follow the children outside, looking up to see the beautiful deep forest green Tharassas displays for us in the evenings, just after sunset. The two moons are already up,

Tarsis chasing Pellin across the sky like a couple of playful children. I wonder, idly, if one will ever catch the other.

"They love spending time with you, you know." Merwyn, my youngest daughter and my pride and joy, appears at my side.

I chuckle, an old man's laugh. "They're not so bad when they sit still." I am famous for my temper, but I try not to show it to the children. Another thing about old age, you become crotchetier with every passing year.

Our camp is an orinth's nest of activity. In two more days, we'll set off to the Gather, where all of the *ce'faine* from the various tribes will meet to trade and exchange stories. The name is an evolution of my own, one I am far more comfortable with than the nickname my mother used to use for me, now a bastardization and a curse among the Heartlanders.

Every now and again, someone new joins us, bringing us news from that faraway land.

"Are you sure they're ready for the rest of this particular tale?" Merwyn puts a hand on my shoulder as if in reassurance, but I know she is worried I will fall if I stand in one place for too long.

I snort. *I might be old, but I'm not that old.* "Yes. They need to know the truth, and they should learn it while they're young. We may feel safe here now, but someday that will change, and they ought to be ready for it."

Merwyn sighs. It's an old argument between us. She thinks we left the Heartland behind, and can live as we please. Oh, how I wish she was right about that.

But she hasn't lived the struggles that I did. She doesn't know what it took to get to this place.

I am glad of that, mostly. It's a beautiful thing, to have grown up without all that anger and terror my generation lived with every day. But we must never forget it.

She chooses not to fight me over it, and instead gives me a big hug. "I love you, Papa." She kisses me on the cheek and squeezes my hand. "Come over to our tent. Jovyn brought down an *ix* this morning, and he's roasting it over the fire as we speak."

I nod and smile and allow myself to be led to her place. We are nomadic people now, with no place to call home, which means all these lands are our home. We wander them from season to season, getting to know them and visiting them again like old friends. *It's a good life.*

And tonight, it's enough to spend the evening with family, eating barbecued *ix*, laughing and sharing stories around the warmth of fire.

JULI

T he next afternoon, after their chores are done, all the children are back in my tent eager to hear the rest of the story. Even my daughter Merwyn is there, sitting at the back cross-legged, with Ellya on her lap.

Ioyo is right up front again with Onley. I see the spark between them and smile, wondering if it will grow into something stronger once the boys are a little older. Love in all its forms makes me happy.

I take my seat and hold my hands out palms up, to my little audience. "I believe I promised you the rest of the story…"

I WAS UP EARLY the next morning, getting water from the well for my Aunt Milena's—Millie for short—household. I didn't know how long we would be staying there, but my mother was determined to make a good impression.

My father and his sister had not had the best relationship, but family was family. She had taken us in without question when we'd appeared on her doorstep in the middle of the night, bedraggled and weary.

It was just after dawn now and the streets were quiet. There had been a lot of raucous noise during the night, including the clamoring bells of the Guard as they were called out to quell the unrest. Mama had held me in her arms the rest of the night. We were all crammed into a small bedroom together that was even smaller than ours back home, and she'd been as scared as I was. It had been a long time since I was allowed in my parents' bed.

The wells were running low, and I had to lower the bucket a long way to reach the water below.

I marveled at how empty the street was. It was rare that I was up at this time in the morning anymore. I had Gully Town almost to myself, except for a few drunks stumbling home after a night at the pub, and some early risers heading to work.

What happened to the Angel? To Joliver? Did he get away? Up close, he'd seemed so human. I always pictured Angels as superior beings, something almost supernatural.

But if he was, did that mean I was supernatural too?

A distant roar shattered my introspection.

I looked up to see the ship lifting off in the distance, from the landing field. I stared at it, my mouth agape. My mouth rarely seemed to be closed in those days.

At first it rose slowly, lifted on a plume of flame, the smoke rolling out across the field mostly hidden by the intervening buildings. My aunt lived on Eagle Spine, not far from where the ship had landed, so I had a good view.

Then it began to ascend more quickly, shaking the ground beneath my feet.

Doors around the square opened, disgorging people who looked up into the bright green sky to watch it go.

The ship wasn't scheduled to leave for three more days. Its

abrupt departure had to be connected to what had happened last night.

Joliver had made it back to the ship, maybe beaten severely by the mob, and they had decided to abandon us all.

I held back my tears. I'd never have the chance to ask him all those questions, but I couldn't blame them. I wouldn't have stayed on this world if I didn't have to. Even without the crippling drought, it was a horrible place to live.

As the ship dwindled to a small speck and then finally vanished into the morning sky, I pulled the bucket up and hurried back to my aunt's house, ignoring the frowns and stares of her neighbors.

Aunt Millie had a cheery fire going in the hearth and was cooking up a pot of breakfast oats for herself and her guests with some of her precious water. She lived alone—she always claimed that she'd never "found the right man."

I don't think she wanted any man, or any woman. She was entirely self-sufficient, and pleasant enough to be around from the few times I had met her, short and stout and usually cheerful. She took in sewing commissions and alterations to make a living. She was quite good at it, working for some of the richest families on Peregrine Spine.

"Just set that down in the corner." She smiled at me. "It's nice to wake up to some company in the house." Her house was twice the size of ours, with four rooms on two floors, quite a luxury for a single woman.

"Thank you for taking us in." Mama had made me promise to be on my best behavior.

"He's very polite, that son of yours," she said to her sister-in-law, who sat next to the fireplace, darning socks. Mama was determined to pull her weight while she was a guest in Aunt Millie's home.

My father had yet to make an appearance, but I could hear him in the flat's bathroom.

I bobbed my head, embarrassed. "Thank you, Aunt Milena."

"Call me Millie." She flashed me a warm smile.

"I try to set a good example, and his father provides the necessary… incentives when needed."

I blushed. I hadn't been spanked since I was a child. "The ship is gone."

Mama nodded. "We could hear it from in here." She closed her eyes, and for just a moment I could see the pain she was holding inside.

I was just about to reply when there was a sharp knock on the door. I tensed, remembering the night before.

Aunt Millie didn't seem at all concerned. "Go get that. I've got to tend to breakfast."

I did as I was told, opening the door nervously.

An older woman as white as my aunt stood there on the doorstep. She looked up at me and frowned.

"You must be Millie's nephew." The frown was gone as quickly as it had appeared, replaced by a too-friendly smile.

I nodded. "And you are…?"

"I'm Elena, one of Millie's best clients. May I come in? I brought her some work." She held up a torn shirt. "It's my son. He gets into these scuffles, and last night he got himself up to no good."

I wondered if last night's *scuffle* had involved someone like me. I shuddered and called out. "Aunt Millie, there's a woman named Elena here, should I let her in?"

"Come on in, El. I have my family visiting me today." The way she said the last word made it sound like it would be a short visit.

I hoped we could go home too, but I wasn't looking forward to being back in the old neighborhood. Not with the likes of Sam'Ost around.

I opened the door and my aunt's friend stepped inside, touching my cheek as she passed. "Thank you, son."

I bristled at that but said nothing.

"Fancy a bit of breakfast while you're here?" My aunt asked, always the consummate host.

Elena made herself right at home, sitting at the table and pushing aside my mother's work. "No thank you, but I wouldn't mind a little wine, if you have it. I didn't sleep a wink last night, with all the commotion."

My aunt had a lot of chairs, part of owning a business I supposed.

"Quite a mess it was. The Guard rounded up a bunch of miscreants and put them in one of the wine cellars for holding."

My ears perked up. Maybe she had news about Joliver.

"Here you go. Traded with the vintners at the end of the spine for it." Aunt Millie handed her a cup of wine, and then served out breakfast portions of the oats for the rest of us.

I sat down and dug into mine eagerly. Aunt Millie was an excellent cook, she must've gotten some special spices from the latest run, because I tasted something I've never had before.

"What's in this? It's delicious." I licked my lips, trying to get every last bit of it.

Millie smiled and petted my shoulder. "It's called *cinnamon*. I traded a couple dresses of my own design for it. The Angels seemed fascinated by the beading."

Elena nodded. "And rightly so. You do beautiful work." She didn't look to be one of my aunt's richer clients, but she must've been doing well enough, from the nice clothes that she wore. She sipped her wine contentedly. "One of the Angels came into town last night," she said casually.

My mother met my gaze, and a slight smile crossed her face. We both knew women like Elena. They gathered gossip like a skerit gathers shiny things, and couldn't wait to show it off to everyone they knew.

"What happened?" My mother sounded perfectly innocent.

"He visited someone up on Red Hawk Spine... say, isn't that where you live?" Elena stared at me.

I nodded. "Yes, but we didn't see anything. We were here for the night." I prayed to the gods that Aunt Millie would back me up.

Elena's gaze shifted to my aunt, who nodded. Disappointment settled over her features at not unearthing another nugget of potential gossip to share among her friends. "In any case, it was the beautiful one. Tall, dark, and handsome, as they say." Her eyes narrowed. "In fact, he looks a fair amount like you."

I shrugged. "I wouldn't know. I didn't see him." I lied through my teeth. I was dying to know what had happened to him, but I didn't want to seem *too* eager. We'd had no other news since we came to Aunt Millie's house. And now the ship was gone, carrying him with it back home to Earth. *I'll never see him again.*

The taste of cinnamon turned to ash on my tongue.

"Well in any case, my friend Elsa over on Red Hawk Spine says they cornered him in a cul-de-sac on Peregrine Spine, and started to beat him." She shook her head. "Men are such hotheaded fools. It was right in front of a guard station."

I wondered if her son had been one of those *fools*. I closed my eyes, feeling pain grip my guts. *How dare they do this to him?* It happened often enough to the rest of us, though it was usually covered up. People who looked like me, and others who just didn't look enough like *them,* usually took the brunt of it. "So they took him back to the ship?" For his sake, I hoped that was true.

She shook her head. "That's the strangest thing." She took another sip of her wine, stretching out the drama while Aunt Millie began to mend her son's shirt. "Elsa says they took him to the clinic, down on Raven Spine. Apparently he's still there." She paused as if for dramatic effect." Do you think he's a criminal, or something?"

I was on my feet before I knew it, fists balled at my sides. "Why would you say that?" I was tired of pretending to be nice to people like her.

Elena went pale. "It's just... Otherwise, why would they leave him?"

My mind was going in a hundred directions at once. I was angry at her for a casual assumption that Joliver was a criminal. I was dumbfounded that he was still here, after his ship had left. And I was worried that more harm might come to him. If he was even still alive. All I said was, "That's interesting." I sat back down, wondering what it all meant.

My aunt must've felt the tension in the room. She finished up the shirt and handed it over to her "friend." "That will be three pieces."

Elena raising eyebrow. "Your rates have gone up."

Aunt Millie smirked. "My work is now known on an interstellar level." She took the money from Elena and immediately helped her up, rushing her out the door. "You'd better hurry home. I'm sure your son needs you, after his... activities last night."

"See you next week." Elena seemed a little flustered at being glad-handed, but it was clear my aunt didn't care.

"Next week then." She closed the door firmly on Elena's face.

I've never loved my aunt more than I did just then. I looked at my mother and aunt, afraid to say it, afraid not to. "We have to help him."

Papa chose that time to arrive at breakfast. "Help who?" He sat down and scooped up his bowl, finishing his helping in three large spoonfuls. "This is delicious, Millie. What's in it?"

"Cinnamon," My mom and I said at once.

"Cimmanin?" My father laughed. "You and your mother are like two mur in a pod. But who are we helping?"

Aunt Millie sat down next to him. "I think they mean the Angel."

I had to go after the Angel, but I couldn't do it on my own. I knew that, even though I wanted to. I hoped my family would see things the same way I did. "We have to go get him."

My father surprised me by nodding. "He's not safe where he is, and his friends have left him behind."

I stared at him, shocked. I had expected resistance to my plan. It was a stupid one, really not much of a plan of all: *Go to the clinic and get him.*

He met my gaze. "What? He's *family.*"

Aunt Millie nodded. "You have to protect your kin."

I guess that shouldn't have surprised me. We were the only family we had. But I wasn't prepared for what came next.

"This is stupid. What are you going to do, just walk in and get him?" Mama was staring at us like we had lost our collective minds. "And then what? Bring him back here? Take him back *home*, where they came to get him in the first place?"

"But mama… he's a part of this family." *Or he could be.* Even Aunt Millie saw that much.

"Maybe so, but he left us. He abandoned my mother, fifty years ago. And he knew what he was doing when he came to see us. He took a chance to salve his own conscience, and it put all of us in jeopardy." She rubbed the back of her neck, like she always did when something really bothered her.

"We could leave." I hadn't meant to say it, but it just popped out. The idea had been percolating in my head for years, that feeling of wanting to be *anywhere but here.*

Everyone turned to look at me as if I was crazy.

"There's no place in the Heartland that isn't like this," my father said evenly. "And some places are far worse." I could tell he understood where I was coming from, but there was a deep sadness in his voice.

"Your father's right." My mother put her hands in her lap, staring at them as if they might hold answers. "I can't count the number of times I wanted to leave this place, but there's nowhere else to go."

I pounded the table, startling all three of them. "But what if there was?"

They stared at me. It would have been comical if not for the deadly earnestness of the conversation.

Finally my mother opened her mouth. "Where?"

I had never heard a single word contain so much hope and fear, all at once. "The Highlands."

The silence was shattered as all three broke into frenetic conversation.

"No one lives there."

"It's too far. How would we get there?"

"Doesn't it get cold in the winters?"

"How would we eat?"

We? The last one was from Aunt Millie. Of the three, she was the last one I would've expected to be supportive. She didn't look like me or mama *at all,* and she had a comfortable life here. "You would go with us?"

She snorted. "Of course I'd go with you. You're my only family." She sighed. "Not that we're going anywhere." She looked at my father, who nodded.

"We don't have the resources to mount an expedition like that. Besides, just the four of us? We wouldn't have a chance." He bit his lip. "Would we?"

"Hmmmm."

Everyone turned to look at mama.

"What?" My father took her hand. His light skin against hers had always seemed the perfect match.

"Not that I'm saying this makes any sense at all. Because it's a crazy idea." She closed her eyes. The pain of a lifetime lived in Gully Town was evident in the wrinkles on her face. I didn't know it then, but she had lived a very difficult life as the daughter of an Angel. Harder than mine, even. "What if it wasn't just us?"

It was my turn to stare. "What do you mean?"

She looked at me thoughtfully. "How many of *us* are there? Children, grandchildren, great grandchildren of Angels, each different from them? There must be hundreds. And every one of them that I know hates it here."

My father squeezed her hand again. "You're talking a mass exodus."

She nodded, warming to her own idea. "How many of us work at the fringes of society, cleaning their homes, taking care of their children, fixing their mistakes?" On that one, she looked directly at my aunt. "You may look like them, but you understand exactly what I mean."

Aunt Millie nodded. Her last client had been proof of that.

"So this isn't just some stupid idea I cooked up in my head?" I couldn't believe they were actually taking me seriously.

"Oh it's a stupid idea. Absolutely." Papa grinned. "Then again, some of the best ideas are. I look like them too, and *I am* sick of living here." He pulled my mother in close for a hug.

Her brow was furrowed. "Your father's right. This is a stupid idea." My mother closed her eyes again and was silent for a long time.

I held my breath, waiting.

At long last, she opened them, looking directly at me. "I am tired of living like this too. I need something to give me hope, so I say yes, let's try your stupid plan."

We set about putting it in action. Papa would go back to the house and collect what was left of our things.

Mama would spread the word among her friends, asking them to meet us at the clinic at nightfall.

Even Aunt Millie had a part to play. She knew folks who had friends in the Guard, and would reach out to find a few of them who would be there to protect us, just in case things went badly. The Guard was supposed to be impartial, but it had a long history of favoring the rich and powerful over the rest of us.

I'd read some of Earth's dark past, and not much had changed since we came here. The long arc of history sometimes snaps and knocks you back down where you came from.

I was going to go out and contact some of my friends. Over the years, I'd met a number of others like myself, and we had formed a loose connection. I was sure they could talk to their families and convince them to come.

Papa vetoed the idea immediately. "Absolutely not. You're not leaving his house until we get back."

Mama crossed her arms and stood next to papa, with that *don't you dare cross me* look on her face. "Your father's right. It's not safe. They know who you are, and I will not have you beaten up by that mob. Or worse." Now that she had warmed to my idea, she seemed to have taken it over as her own.

"But mama…" What was I supposed to do? Just sit here on my hands all day long?

"No buts. If I come back and you're not here, I'll…"

I manage a slight smile. "What? Banish me to the bedroom?"

Her face softened. She leaned forward and kissed me on the cheek. "Please just stay here, Charlie. I need to know you're safe." Coming from her, the word still sounded sweet.

I stared at her, defeated. How could I say no to her? "Sure, Mama."

And then they were all gone.

As the morning wore on into afternoon, I debated sneaking out, seeing my friends, and getting back to Aunt Millie's before they returned. But I'd made a promise to her, and I'd never broken one of those before. So, instead I paced the room, waiting for them to come back.

I still couldn't believe that they'd all gone along with my mad plan, but then again, they had lived in this world much longer than me.

After a while I got tired of pacing. I sat down on a cushion in one of the corners, closed my eyes, and tried to remember everything I had learned about the Highlands.

They were beyond the Heartland, far to the east, accessible through a narrow gap that threaded the way between Heaven's Reach and the Red Flight Mountains. It would be a long trek, especially with so many people—assuming that anyone else would go along with it. My head spun with all the things that could go wrong.

There was a sharp knock at the door.

I sprang up, looking wildly around, and remembering that I was the only one there. Should I stay quiet and pretend the house was empty?

Whoever it was knocked again. "Charlie, you in there?"

I knew that voice, though I hadn't heard it in years. "Juli?"

She sounded annoyed. "Yes, you idiot. Let me in."

I unbolted the door and opened it to stare at her. She looked the same, only older, her long blonde hair pulled back and tied with a leather thong. She was dressed much as I was, in homeweave shirt and pants, and yet she somehow made them look almost fashionable. "Get inside. Someone might see you."

She slipped through the narrow space, and I closed the heavy door behind her and turned to stare at her. "What are you doing here?" It was good to see a friend again.

She returned my stare. "I heard what you're doing," she said at last.

I braced for the worst. "I'm not doing anything but being locked up in my aunt's house." It was the truth, and it still rankled me.

"You know what I mean. About the exodus."

My eyes went wide. "How did you hear?"

"My uncle Jos. He's..."

I had met her uncle once. His grandfather had been an angel too. "You can say it. He's like me."

She nodded, looking relieved. "He said... he said you're all going to leave."

I stared at her. I wasn't sure I could trust her, though she'd defended me when I was little. "How did you find me?" And who else might know we were here?

She must have seen the look of fear on my face. "Don't worry. You brought me here once with your family, when you came to visit your aunt. I tried your old house first... Charlie, I'm so sorry."

I frowned. "Sorry for what?"

She stared at me again, unnerving me. "You don't know?"

"Juli, just tell me." Waiting was often worse than knowing.

"They burned down your house, Charlie." She looked away. "It took out three other homes with it, before they could put out the fire."

Holy green hell. Is papa okay? My mouth gaped open. Again. "When? Did anyone...?" I swear I didn't want to, but I wished in that moment that Sam'Ost, the neighbor who had come after my grandfather, had died in the fire.

Julie shook her head. "I don't know. Early this morning, I think. I didn't stick around to find out. May I?" She pointed at one of Aunt Millie's chairs.

"Of course." I was trying to absorb the news that the place I'd grown up, my family's home for generations, was gone. It hadn't been much, but it was ours.

She sat down with a heavy sigh. "Charlie, I want to go with you. A lot of us do."

"But... you're..."

She looked at her white arm. "Yes, I am. With brown eyes. Not blue."

I stared at her. Such a small thing. Surely it wasn't enough to make a difference. But I knew better.

Does it matter? Some of us were brown, a few lighter, a few darker. Some had a golden glow to their features. Some had red hair, some brown. And many of us had brown eyes. "But what about your family?"

"It's just my dad and my uncle, and my father doesn't care one whit about me. He always says he's embarrassed about his daughter with the *throwback eyes.*"

I whistled. The older I got, the more I realized how much I disliked other people. And who was I, to choose who could go and who couldn't? "Why not?"

This was quickly turning from a late-night escape to a revolution.

What would Gully Town do without all of her cooks and cleaners and menders? On the other hand, we'd have all the skills we needed to create our own world in the Highlands.

I was becoming more and more convinced that we just had to reach out and grab it.

CHEFAINE

The streets of Eagle Spine were quiet that evening when we left my aunt's house. Eerily quiet, though there was a dull roar in the distance.

I looked uneasily at my mother and father, wondering what it meant.

Each of us had a large carry sack strapped to our backs, with everything we planned to take with us. It wasn't much.

My father had traded in most of our belongings—the ones we'd brought to Aunt Millie's house the night before—for things that we would need on the road, including dried rations that would get us through a week or so. I had no concept then how hard it would be.

When he'd returned safely from our house to report on the damage, I'd thrown my arms around him, determined to never let him go.

Now, we trudged down the street together, approaching the bridge the connected Eagle Spine to Raven Spine. As we turned onto the narrow roadway that led to it, the noise grew louder.

A couple of young men, more typical of the population of

Gully Town than we were, passed us and sneered at us. "Go back home."

One of them spat at us.

My father had to restrain me from throwing myself at them. "It's not worth it. Let it go."

I turned to my mother, but she nodded.

"Listen to your father. This will all be over soon enough."

They had always chosen the way of peace, and I have always respected them for that. But just then, I really wanted to hit someone.

The men laughed and walked away. "Cowards."

I started off after them, but my mother pulled me back.

She took my cheeks in her hands. "Listen to me, Charlie. Joliver needs us. And I need you."

That last part stopped me cold. What would mama do without me? Without my papa, should something happen to him? She was strong and so was he, but the three of us were strongest together. "Mama…"

"Let it go."

I closed my eyes and took a deep breath. "All right." *This will all be over soon.*

We crossed the bridge and descended into a nightmare. People lined the streets, a crowd that looked nothing like me. They were angry mutterings, and people stared at me as if they had never seen someone with skin like mine. That was aurshit, of course. We lived among them, doing work for them every single day. But we might as well have been invisible.

Not today. I wondered how my father and aunt felt, walking there with us, feeling the same harsh stares that we felt all the time. They *knew*—how could they not?—but *knowing* and *feeling* are two different things.

The four of us bunched together unconsciously, bound by the hostility of the crowd. We were not alone, however. Other groups of people were also making their way down the road toward the old City Hall, the Guard House, and the Clinic—the oldest part of Gully Town, built soon after the Landing. There was a sense of history in the air, both from those landmarks and from what was happening today.

I've never seen people like me—my people—stand up and demand to be respected.

My anger shifted to something different, something stronger. It took me a minute to recognize it, as alien as it was to me. *Pride.*

Blue wisps floated above the scene as if they were following us, borne by the sprightly ocean breeze.

As we approached the heart of the Old Quarter around Founder's Square, the composition of the crowd changed. Suddenly there were more people around me with dark skin, more who were not as white as an inthym. People with hair of all different hues, of eyes that sparkled in brown and hazel and green. They were chanting something together, but at first it was hard to make out what they were saying.

People reached out to me as I passed, touching me, squeezing my arms, pulling at the hem of my shirt.

"It's him." Whispers spread through the crowd.

I looked around, confused at what was happening. *How did these people know me?*

And then I saw the first sign.

A little girl of about five years old, holding up a thick piece of hencha paper with my image on it—a painting of me, clearly reproduced on a printing press, with the words "I am *different.*"

My heart caught in my throat at the site. I turned to look at mama. "Did you know about this?"

She shook her head. She reached out to touch my cheek, her eyes wet. "I'm so proud of you, Charlie."

Her voice was swallowed up by the crowd, but I heard it. The sense of pride in my chest swelled. No matter what else happened tonight, this had been worth it.

And at last I understood what the crowd was chanting.

"Release the fallen angel! Release the fallen angel! Release the fallen angel!"

They said it over and over again, in unison. I joined in, shaking my fist in the air with each call.

We reached the steps to the clinic, and the crowd pressed in, hundreds strong. *Where did they all come from?*

I'd had no idea there were so many of us in Gully Town. *We're not alone.*

My *stupid* idea had inspired a movement, and suddenly I was scared of what would happen. It was all spinning out of control. What if someone got hurt?

I hadn't meant for any of this to happen. I'd just wanted to come here, free Joliver, and get out of town. I'd hoped that— at best—a few dozen people might come with us to start a life somewhere else. Honestly, I hadn't got any farther than that. I was climbing the stairs ahead of them and my mind was blank. Here I was, my name on a poster, a crowd waiting breathlessly for me to say… *something.*

I stopped on the second to the last step.

The chant died down to nothing, and an eerie silence filled the square, broken only by the sound of the wind as it whistled in from the Harkness Sea, a few hundred meters to my right, and down Grindell Lane.

The clinic's heavy flopwood doors were closed. I stared them for a moment, uncertain what to do.

The energy from the crowd was like a living thing. I could feel it flickering, hope becoming consternation as all the gathered people watched me hesitate. It was a strange thing, knowing that so much depended on what I did next.

Mama put her hand on the space between my shoulder blades and leaned over to whisper in my ear. "Speak to them. Speak from your heart." She could feel it too.

I swallowed hard and nodded. Turning my back on the

clinic, I looked out at the hushed crowd and spoke the first words that came to mind.

"Ever since I was little, I've felt like I don't belong here in Gully Town. No one else is like me. No one understood me."

They were murmurs of assent in the crowd.

"I spend every day looking over my shoulder, wondering what they're saying about me, wondering what will happen next." I looked over at my papa.

He nodded.

I took a deep breath, and went on, my voice becoming stronger, more certain. "Then an Angel fell out of the sky. At the landing, a man stepped out of that ship who looked just like me." I remembered the sparkle in his eyes, the easy confidence. "He looks like me not only because of his skin, but because he's my grandfather."

There were confused whispers now, as the crowd digested what I was saying.

"The Angel inside those walls has a name." I pointed at the doors behind me, jabbing my finger at them. "It's Joliver Eckston. He's a man, just like us." I give that a second to sink in. "And as we found out last night, he can be hurt, just like us."

My father put his arm around my shoulder and squeezed me tight.

As I looked out into the crowd, I realized there were more than a few faces like his—like the blond, blue-eyed, white-skinned Gullanders who had looked down on me my entire life—only this time, they were looking up at me, and nodding.

"I am tired of being hurt. Aren't you?"

"Speak!" The call went up from a number of folks in the crowd.

"I'm tired of being tired." Every slur, every dirty look, every rock thrown at me came back to me. All the pain surging in my chest. "Aren't you?"

"Yes!" This time it was a full-throated chorus.

I blinked. They were listening to me. Really listening. "My grandfather comes from a place where being different doesn't change how others look at you." I didn't know that for certain, but I was fairly sure from what Joliver had told us that it was true. "Where what you can do is not limited by who you are."

The crowd muttered in agreement. I could see the guards stationed along the periphery of the square shifting nervously in place. I hope some of them were friends.

When my audience quieted down, I continued. "We mean no harm to our fellow Gullanders. But we are tired of being treated this way. We are tired of doing all the work and getting none of the credit. We are tired of being beaten in the streets in the middle of the night while the Guard looks the other way."

The crowd was with me. I could feel their energy surging in my bones.

"We will liberate the Angel—my grandfather—and together we will leave this place. Together we will make a new home where no one is judged for how they look. Together we will make our own way in the world and leave this sad city to struggle on without us!"

The crowd roared and there was thunderous applause. A thrill went up my spine again—a startling mix of fear and potential. We could do this. *I can do this.*

And suddenly I knew what I had been put on this world for.

I put my hand in the air, palm out, and the crowd went quiet once more. We stared at each other for a moment, all those people and me, and I closed my eyes and nodded. We didn't have *emps* back then, but I knew what they felt, and they knew my heart.

I turned and climbed the last step and crossed the open area at the top of the stairs to the closed doors. I knocked three times, and the world waited to see what would happen next. "Release the fallen angel!" *Joliver. My grandfather.*

There was a long silence.

I stared at the door, willing it to open, feeling the energy start shifting again behind me as the crowd became restless.

What if it didn't open?

What if the crowd surged forward and broke the doors down?

Or worse, what if everyone just gave up and went home?

Then I heard the sound of a lock being undone, a latch being turned.

I half expected violence, half expecting to be told politely to go away. The world balanced on a knife edge as we collectively held our breath.

The door swung open, and Joliver stood there, flanked by two medics in white coats.

I stared at him, almost not recognizing him.

His face was a mess, bruised and swollen, his left eye almost squeezed shut. He looked tired, broken, a shadow of the Angel I'd seen descend from the ship out on the landing field.

Then he smiled, and I knew it was him.

I threw my arms around his waist and squeezed him tight, and mama joined me. "You're all right?" Her voice cracked.

"Careful around the ribs." He winced, and we let go. "I took a little damage, but you should see the other guy." That grin lit his face again.

A cheer went up behind us. I turned to see them surging up the stairs—not in anger, but in joy. The mood was transformed, as if it were a festival day. Everyone crowded around the five of us, and together we laughed and cried.

I pulled Joliver aside and whispered into his ear. "Your ship left you."

He nodded. "I know. I told them to. It wasn't safe for them to stay."

I pondered that. Would Earth decide that we were too much of a risk, and stop sending supplies? Was Tharassas ready for that?

What would we do when the flitters broke down? When fine metals no longer came to us on neatly wrapped pallets? When my aunt would never be able to get cinnamon again?

I supposed we would find out.

I stared at him in wonder. "So you decided to stay?"

He nodded. "This is where my family is." He winced again, whether from the pain of his injuries or the ache in his heart, I didn't know. "I should never have left, all those years ago."

I was grateful that he had. Otherwise I might never have known him. I looked out at the gathered crowd. "Will you come with us?"

He raised an eyebrow. "Where are you going?"

"We're leaving Gully Town for the Heartland. If we can reach it."

He grinned, and I saw mama in his features, the way he looked at me, for just a moment. "Lead on, and I will follow. I have maps in my head that will help." He put a hand on my shoulder. "I am so proud of you… grandson."

I laughed. It was strange to hear that word from a man just a few years older than me.

A twirling of wisps chose that moment to spin around us and ascend into the green sky. A sky that was growing cloudier as I watched.

I turned to the crowd, and lifted up my arm with his, hand in hand.

A hush spread from me, down the stairs and across the square. The sea of faces looked up at me once again.

"It's time. Gather your things, and follow us to the promised land." I don't know where that came from, but it just seemed right, in the moment. "The Angel will come with us."

I took my mother's hand with my free one, and my aunt and father flanked us as we moved down the stairs.

The people parted, letting us pass as if we were royalty.

We marched up the street, leading the rest of the crowd down the cobblestone road. The gathered denizens of Gully Town jeered, throwing rotten fruit at us, calling us names, but a strange peace had fallen over the crowd.

They could insult us. They could laugh at us. They could even hit us. But they could no longer hurt us.

We crossed over to Peregrine Spine, briefly walking among the houses of the rich of the city as we crossed the narrow strip of land before going across another bridge and reaching Red Hawk Spine, the last of the islands that comprised Gully Town.

The angry mob faded behind us.

At last, we came to Landing Bridge, our gateway to freedom. Beyond was the landing field and then the open roads of the Heartland, and a long ways off in the distance, the Highlands.

I looked at mama and papa and they both smiled and nodded.

Juli and her uncle were behind me. She flashed me a bright smile.

I looked at Joliver. He pointed the way.

"From here on out, it is up to you to lead the *different*." He must have read it on the signs.

It was strange for me to hear that name applied to all of the people who surrounded me. It filled my heart with pride. And yet, it had been used against me so many times before.

I climbed the arch of the bridge, feeling the stiff wind that was now blowing from the west. I turned to address the people—my people—one last time before we left the city that has been both our home and our prison.

"From now on, we will call ourselves the chefaine." *Faine* was an old word, a name I'd run across once, that meant "joyous," and che meant *that* or *those* in another old language. We would be sad no more.

"Long live the chefaine." Joliver held up his fist.

The crowd echoed him. "Long live the chefaine."

In less than a day, we had gone from being outcasts to finding a shared identity, becoming a people, brought together by our mutual persecution.

The first drops fell as we crossed the bridge, a warm, life-giving rain that promised to finally end the drought.

I took my mother's hand with my left and Joliver's with my right, and together we crossed the bridge with the rain, leaving Gully Town to find a new life.

I OPENED MY EYES. I remember that moment as if it were yesterday. So many things have happened since, moments of great joy and moments of towering sorrow, like when my firstborn died when he was only two.

Ellya is looking up at me. She reaches up to touch the stubble on my cheek.

I've grown lazy over the last few years, only shaving once a week. When you get old, your priorities change, and keeping up my personal appearance beyond the necessary was no longer one of mine.

"What happened after you left Gully Town?"

That was another story. A long, hard journey through a hostile land, two months of travel that would eventually bring us to a new home. So I answer the best I can.

"You happened. You and your brother Ioyo and his friends, and your mother Merwyn and all the rest. You are the end of that long journey."

My mother and father, Joliver, and even my Aunt Millie all took their own Long Trek over the years, passing away from life into memory.

When I close my eyes, though, I can still feel them with me.

I am the only one left of my family who remembers those days. I will follow in their footsteps soon, before too many more turnings of the world.

I squeeze Ellya tight, proud of what we did, and content that my children and grandchildren will pick up the tale from here. "You are my bright hope. You are the ce'faine now."

THE LAST RUN

274 AL

The events of The Last Run take place in 274 AL (After Landing), 143 years before the Tharassas Cycle, and describe the final cargo run from Earth to Tharassas. A little over a hundred years after the events of The Fallen Angel, much has changed in the Heartland, including Gully Town, now called Gullytown, but much is still the same...

INBOUND

Sera's back arched as she gulped a lungful of air, her eyes bulging out of their sockets. She collapsed back on the memory foam of her sleep pod, sucking oxygen into her lungs gratefully.

It was a bit stale, but not immediately fatal—a good sign given how they escaped near-certain destruction by the skin of their teeth, as Earth and her local colonies fell into chaos and self-imposed destruction.

Sera's throat was raw, dry—the antiseptic spray either hadn't worked or hadn't been administered by the *Spin Diver's* wake-up protocols. "Waaaater."

A slim white feeder line slipped down from above to mouth level. She took the sipper between her lips and sucked in the gloriously wet liquid.

Like the air, it tasted a bit off. She sighed. *Time enough to figure that out later.*

She drank her fill and sat up, swinging her feet off the edge of the couch to look around the sleep room.

The other three pods were dark.

"Tavi!" Sera slipped off the couch and winced. Every one of her muscles ached.

She hobbled her way to the closest pod. *Please—no.*

It felt like just minutes before—when their fingers had been intertwined, Tavi giving her a quick kiss as the ship shuddered all around them, the air filling with noxious smoke. Staring at each other as the hardened plas lids slid closed over them.

Sera fumbled with the manual release controls on Tavi's pod, frantic. They were unresponsive, as dark as the pod itself.

Sera stumbled to the wall and retrieved the axe that was strapped there for emergencies. She managed to lift it up, her shoulder muscles on fire from the weight. She brought it down blade-first on the plas cover of the dark sleep pod. The reinforced plas cracked but didn't break.

She lifted the axe again and brought it down hard on the slick surface.

The axe blade skittered across the smooth shell, and the handle slipped out of her grasp. The axe fell on the metallic floor on the far side of the pod with a loud clatter in the deceleration-created gravity.

Sera squeezed past the pod to retrieve it, sparing a quick glance for the two unoccupied pods.

Jace and Herrol hadn't even made it to the ship. They were long dead by now.

Sera lifted the axe once more and brought it down on the cover with all her weakened strength.

The plas shattered at last, revealing the pod's contents.

The musky smell of decay slammed into Sera, driving her back toward the exit hatch. She couldn't believe that it was true—that Tavi was long dead, her corpse a shrunken mess of bones and dried flesh.

"Oh God." Sera stumbled backward and slammed her hand on the hatch release. She practically fell through it, slamming her hand on the door control outside.

It spiraled closed, shutting off the horrible sight, but leaving the sickly-sweet smell lingering in the air.

Sera fell to her knees and retched.

After almost twenty-five years in suspension, there was nothing left in her to come out, but still her stomach heaved. It was a primal reaction, far beyond her ability to control. *She's gone.*

Then she just lay there, wrecked and broken. "Tavi." *How did this happen?*

Time slowed and dilated.

Her mind refused to process what she had just seen. It was too visceral, too real.

Too painful.

She closed her eyes and sobbed.

JAS'AYA STOOD UP AND STRAIGHTENED, rubbing her back where the muscles knotted and ached from the hard work in the field.

Around her, the purple rows of hencha plants stretched out into the distance, their red stalks moving of their own accord even when there was no breeze.

Her shoulder sack was full of hencha berries teased from the semi-sentient plant—red, orange and blue spheres that emitted the most delicious scent.

If she closed her eyes, she could almost hear the murmuring of the plants. They spoke to one another, whispers that drifted tantalizingly out of reach. She wished she could understand what they were saying. Sometimes she felt like she got a word or two, but then it slipped away on the wind that blew steadily up the valley from the Harkness Sea.

She had stopped telling people about her little fantasies. The last time she had mentioned them, she'd gotten in trouble with her shift supervisor and had been put on probation for a week. To the rest of the crew, the hencha were just plants.

Jas dusted off her light blue skirt, the kind all the field workers wore. She needed a break, even if it was just a short one. She pulled her unusually dark hair back behind her ears and set off toward the collector.

The sun was bright green overhead, matched to a sky which was a deeper shade of the same color. It was already past noon—soon they'd be called in for lunch under the welcoming shade of one of the big-leaved flop trees that dotted the plantation.

She was thirsty. It was warm out today and she'd been chewing on a piece of bacca root all morning long to keep her mouth wet. She spat it out—it was reduced to a black, well-gummed wad.

Jas dropped her load of berries into the collector, which hummed happily as it processed them by type.

She waved at Meriam two rows over and took a sip of water from the collector's spigot. It was warm but welcome as it washed away the dust of the farm.

She was ahead of quota—she had a way with the hencha, which responded to her more readily than to most of the other harvesters. If she kept at it, she might earn a bonus day she could spend with her mother at home. Lyn'Aya was sick. Jas didn't know what was wrong with her but it seemed serious—the skin on her arms had strange bumps, and her fingernails were covered with red lines. Her joints ached too —she hardly ever managed a full night's sleep anymore—and her nose bled whenever she sneezed.

Some of the other older women had the same symptoms, but no one seemed to know why.

If she could have, Jas would have stayed at home to care for Lyn'Aya, to keep her as comfortable as possible.

Her mother was a formidable person, stocky and forceful. She had clawed her way up from serfdom to contractor after

Jas had been born and she'd shared all she had learned about their world with her daughter.

Jas returned to the next plant in the row. She knelt, ripping out a heyfa weed that had wrapped itself around the base of the plant. The little yellow thing screamed and twisted in her hand before fading to a pale white and going limp.

She threw it down on the ground and stomped on it until it was flat.

She knelt before the plant and her fingers worked quickly, slipping through the red leaves of the hencha to find the bundle of nerves underneath. Her fingers massaged them gently, and she felt it shiver under her touch.

Silanya. The word slipped into her mind, the name of this particular hencha plant, as closely as she could translate it into the human tongue. They often spoke to her when she harvested their berries, though she didn't always understand them.

Jas'Aya.

Thank you. It wasn't in human words so much as a feeling, a warmth that spread through her mind like the opening of a flower.

Jas felt a shiver of pleasure in the hencha's nerves, both a physical and mental sensation. Then the plant's skin split and a few berries were deposited in her open hand.

She didn't know if the hencha spoke to anyone else. It felt private, something special she shared with the strange alien life form. She was afraid to speak of it to anyone else, lest she be penalized again for her "strange ideas."

She pulled her hand out gently and deposited the berries in her bag. "Thank you."

The hencha rustled as if in reply.

"They're coming!" Cyr's voice carried down the rows of hencha as she ran toward them, the woman's long blond hair flying behind her, her arms waving wildly in the air. "They're coming!"

The women gathered around her as she arrived. Cyr was sweating and out of breath, hands on her knees.

"Who's coming?" Jas had never seen the woman get so worked up.

"Runners from Earth." She grinned, "There's gonna be a Market Day in Gullytown!"

~

HOURS LATER, as the sun dropped toward the horizon, Jas dumped the last of the berries into the collector impatiently, tapping her foot while it sorted the load.

Market Day. The words carried a bit of magic, like a fairy tale that parents told their children that would never actually come true. Still, she wanted to believe in it. The last one had been before she was born, but her mother had told her about it:

The big ships come in with all manner of wonderful items—spices, fabrics and flitter parts and raw materials and medicines that will cure almost anything. There are machines big and small, wondrous dishes and toys and things you never dreamed of. Her mother's eyes had glittered in the firelight, and Jas had imagined buying herself wings from the Runners. Gauzy fairy wings that would carry her wherever she wanted to go.

The runs arrived about once every two decades. This one was already a couple years overdue, but no one seemed to know how they chose their schedules.

Some of her friends had whispered that there would be no more of them, that Earth had surely forgotten her colonies, including little agrarian Tharassas. Some—the Separatists—wished they would never come back at all.

Jas had been entranced by all the stories. There was something amazing and romantic about the idea of traveling between the stars, of traversing the vast distances between planets like modern-day pirates.

Mamma had told her stories about the pirates on the Seven Seas, back on Earth—Lon Jon Siller, the Black Bard…

And now a ship was coming and there would be another Market Day!

"You're a little off today." Jemmy, her supervisor, frowned at the totals on the side of the collector.

"Sorry… I've been sick." *More like daydreaming about Market Day.*

Jemmy nodded. "Just don't let it happen again."

"I won't. Listen…" She put her hand on Jemmy's arm. "I need a day off. Just one."

His bushy brows furrowed. "I don't know. We're in the middle of the harvest. I need you here—"

"It's my mother," she lied. Lyn'Aya *was* sick, but Jas had more on her mind than a day at home. "She's taken a turn for the worse." She looked over her shoulder at the rows of hencha. "I think mamma's close to seed."

Jemmy bit his lip. Hencha plants died when they went to seed. Everyone knew it. "All right. One day. But I need you back here on Martasday."

"Thank you." She threw her arms around him. "You don't know how much this means." She kissed his cheek.

He snorted. "Enough of that. See you day after tomorrow."

Jemmy was a bit skittish about touching, but she couldn't help herself. She was going to Market Day for her mother! "Thank you!" She practically ran to the flit stop, but even though the flitter was there, she had to wait for the others to finish before it could take her home.

The women—blond every last one but her—boarded the little craft, and its rotors spun to lift it silently into the air.

They had long since stopped noticing her differences.

The flitter swerved off to the south toward Corinth, the village where she and the others in her crew lived. The tiny village sat up in the hills, looking over the wide valley where the hencha plantations thrived.

Jas had worked in them all. Each plant could only be harvested once every twenty days, so the workforce continually rotated through the various owners' fields. The plantation owners paid the supervisors and some of that pay—a very small amount—trickled down into her account.

A breeze blew up from Gullytown, making the hencha below sway like a red sea. Even up here, she could smell the plants—they had a bright, sharp, sweet scent that got into her hair and clothing, and had to be washed out at home, but she didn't mind.

The flitter swooped low over the fields, and then caught a warm updraft and soared up into the hills.

"Wish I could go to Gullytown for the Market Day." Myr'Oyl stared off into the distance, down the valley toward the capital. The sun was setting over the ridges there, painting the clouds green and gold.

"Ever been?"

Myr nodded. "I was ten the last time. My papa took me—it took three days to get there on urseback."

"My mamma went before I was born." *Three days to get to Gullytown!* Jas needed a faster way.

Cyr had said the Runners were already inbound. Market Day would likely be in the next day or two. Even if it lasted a week, all the good trade would be gone.

She had an idea. It was a little crazy, and she'd miss more than one day at work, but she was sure she could sweet-talk Jemmy out of a penalty when she returned.

The flitter slipped out of the sky to alight just below the hilltop where the twenty small cottages that made up Corinth perched overlooking the valley. The other women dismounted one by one, heading off to their own homes.

Jas waved farewell to the other field hands. She held back, waiting until they were all gone. "Torry. A moment?" She rested a hand on his shoulder, aware of her impact on him even if she didn't feel the same.

The flitter pilot nodded, running a hand through his blond hair. "What's up?"

"I need a favor."

LYN'AYA

The Spin Diver shook, threatening to break itself into pieces before the ship even reached the planet. It was coming in too hot. Sera had to find a way to dampen her speed before the atmosphere shook it apart.

"Incoming ship, please rep—" The voice was interrupted by a burst of static.

Sera was too busy to pay it any mind.

The ship should have slowed as it entered the Tharassas system. It must have shed at least some of its speed or she would have screamed right through the system and out the other side, headed for who-knew-where. *Thank God it woke me up.*

"Spin, deploy the sail." The solar sail would cut some of Spin Diver's speed.

If only she had an emergency brake.

"Sail deploying." The ship's voice was clinical, sterile.

She and her team hadn't been able to afford a full-on AI when they had taken on the contract, almost a year earlier—twenty-six years earlier if you counted ship suspension time.

By that time, the government was giving them to anyone

with a space-worthy cargo ship. They had even paid for the engine retrofit to prepare the ship for interstellar travel.

Even then, they had known it would be a one-way trip.

Personally, she would have preferred to go to Horus, or maybe Persephone. Tharassas had a *reputation*, as it had been colonized by a purist group that prized genetic homogeneity—a world full of blond-haired blue-eyed automatons. But that had been a couple hundred years before and beggars couldn't be choosers.

From the research she had done, her own sepia-tone skin would be a head turner among the mostly white, mostly blond population.

If only the damned physicists hadn't been right about the infeasibility of FTL travel. They would have been able to get here—or anywhere, really—via warp drive like in the tridees without using the sleep pods and Tavi would still be alive.

Sera choked, thinking about her partner. Her wife. Tavi's ready smile floated in the air before her, the sound of her bubbly, nerdy laugh music to Sera's ears.

Biting her lip hard, she shoved the memory to the back of her mind. *No time for melancholy.*

She checked the velocity and course projection. *Still going too fast.*

She could burn off some fuel to slow herself down, but she was already dangerously low on what she'd need to manage a safe landing on Tharassas.

She needed to do something else.

The cargo. If she could fire enough mass off ahead of her course, it would slow the ship down. *Every action has an equal and opposite reaction.* Basic physics were especially true in space.

"Spin, keep us on the current heading."

"Affirmative."

Sera clambered down the ladder to cargo storage to see what she could do.

Jᴀꜱ ᴍᴀᴅᴇ her way up the hill, weaving through the spiny stone outcrops toward the circle of small one-story, cone-roofed cottages that included her own. They were built from the plentiful black stones of the region and thatched with the red leaves of dead hencha plants.

Once she had dreamed of going to Gullytown, or of becoming an adventurer who would bring back wonders from the nearly unexplored wilds that surrounded the Heartland. Then her father had died, leaving her and her mother all alone, and she had to go to work in the fields to earn enough to support the two of them.

"Mamma! I have news!" She burst through the door into the one-room hovel. "There's gonna be a Market Day!"

Her mother sat by the fireplace, wrapped in a warm blanket made from urse-fur. As Jas entered, Lyn'Aya looked up, her face white as a ghost, her skin was almost translucent. "You're home!" She shifted forward to greet her daughter.

"Don't get up." Lyn'Aya was so weak lately. "Here, I brought you a few berries." She'd snuck them into a hidden pocket of her work shirt, where Jemmy would be unlikely to check.

"The red ones?" Her mother's eyes lit up.

"Yes, Mum." She handed them over and her mother took them greedily in her gnarled hands.

Jas sat next to her on another of the low cushions and watched as Lyn ate them deliberately, one at a time, savoring their tart, sweet flavor.

The scientists said that the hencha had altered their chemistry for the humans in exchange for protection from the heyfa and each of the berries supplied needed nutrients for the human population. How it had happened was a mystery.

Her mother licked her fingers, looking up at Jas hopefully, like a child who'd just finished a sweet.

"No more, sorry."

"That's all right. Thank you." She wiped her hands on the blanket, leaving red stains like blood. "I hate that I am such a burden to you."

"You're no burden." Jas kissed her mother's forehead and got up to make dinner. She had some vegetables she'd purchased at the market square over in Devon, and a few flavor cubes too, made from berries like the ones she picked every day.

She chopped up the tubers and slipped them into a pot of water she'd collected earlier in the morning before going to work. She dropped in a pinch of salt and the cubes, and soon had the meal ready to cook over the fire. "There's going to be a Market Day."

Her mother sat up, her eyes bright. "When? I would love to go to a Market Day again."

"A couple days." She poured a little henchwine, heated in an earthenware jug next to the fire, into two cups. She handed one to her mother and sipped from the other. It warmed her stomach and she could feel it spreading through her like fire. "I still remember you telling me about the last one."

Lyn'Aya nodded. "It was the most amazing day of my life. The men in their ship-suits, white as the driven snow. They were like angels." She sipped her wine, and some of the lines on her face smoothed. "They were so lovely, so different. Dark hair, red hair, brown eyes…"

"I remember. 'Like angels from heaven,' you said." Her mother wasn't religious, following neither the cross nor the sickle, but she *loved* to talk about her angels.

"Yes. They brought us so many things. The most colorful cloth to make dresses from—material that never stained and never wrinkled. Strange, wonderful spices—cinnmen, coomen, garlick—flavors you have never tasted in your life. And the men…"

Jas turned to stare at her mother. *This* was new. "You mean the *angels*?"

Her mother looked like she was far away, staring into the fire as if it were another world. "His name was Jason. He was… beautiful. His skin so soft, not hard like the farmers and tanners and blacksmiths here. He smelled like flowers and the sky…"

Jas frowned. *"Jason?"*

Lyn'Aya's eyes focused and she looked up at Jas. "Yes, dear. Your father."

Jas staggered back against the wooden wall of the cottage. "My father? But you said… you always told me Corvin was my father." Corvin, who had been harder than stone, and about as talkative.

Lyn'Aya frowned. "Did I? That's strange. Your *real* father is probably dead by now. Or married to a nice Earth girl." She sipped a little more wine. It seemed to be loosening her tongue tonight, along with the news of the Run. "Artur convinced me to break it off with him, to stay here in the Heartland. He didn't like them, the Earth men."

"Artur?"

"Mas Vellin. The head of the Council, now."

Jas blinked twice at that one. Her mother had been involved with the Council? How many other secrets had she kept, all these years? *My father?*

Lyn'Aya ran her twisted, aged fingers over her lips. "When Jason left, it almost killed me… I can still remember the taste of him."

Jas stared at her. Did she mean… *Am I the daughter of an angel?* "Jason… was my father? Is that why I'm not blonde, like most folks?"

Lyn'Aya nodded. "He had beautiful, thick dark hair." She grinned like a little girl, her hand clawing the air. "Oh, how I used to love to run my hands through that hair." She sighed, and her hand dropped back down to her lap. "When it got out that I was pregnant with an angel's child… well, they chased me out of Gullytown. I came here, and eventually married Corvin to give you a stable home."

Jas looked away. It was too much to take in all at once. Her whole life was a lie. Everything she believed about her family, her father… Corvin had been an awful man, but at least he had been hers. She wondered if that was why he'd always treated her so coldly.

Daughter of an angel.

Taking a deep breath, she ladled soup into a couple of hand-carved wooden bowls and sank down next to her mother, her mind awhirl with strange thoughts. An awkward silence descended between the two of them.

She sipped her soup, staring at the flickering flames of the fire. "Why haven't you ever told me about this before?" she asked at last.

Lyn shook her head, pushing a wisp of gray hair back behind her ear. "You were too young to understand." She was looking at the fire too, perhaps afraid to meet her daughter's gaze. "I was going to go with him, back to Earth…"

Too much. "I'm taking you with me to Market Day."

Her mother's head whipped around as if she were a woman half her age. "You *can't* leave your job like that. Not for days and days."

Jas took another sip of the soup. "You just let me worry about that."

"But I *have* to—" Whatever she'd been about to say was lost in a coughing fit. They'd been getting worse for weeks.

Jas took her mamma's hands. "It's okay, Mamma. Just breathe." She met her mother's eyes and Lyn'Aya nodded. She took a deep breath, coughed again, and closed her eyes. They breathed slowly together until Lyn'Aya found her balance again.

Jas grabbed the henchwine. "Here, drink some more wine. It will help."

Her mother took the cup gratefully. "Thank you."

"You said the Runners bring medicine. I am going to try to get some for you." She hated seeing her mother like this. Maybe they would have a cure.

"But your job—"

"I *said* let me worry about that."

Lyn'Aya searched her daughter's eyes. "You always were stubborn. Just like your mother." She chuckled and coughed a bit more. Then she pushed herself up to stand unsteadily.

"Mamma—"

Lyn'Aya waved her away. "Oh, let me be. I need to move around a bit." She tottered to the back of the room, opening up her small, hand-carved hope chest. She never shared its contents with her daughter and Jas had never pried, but sometimes she had caught mother fondly looking at something inside.

Lyn'Aya rummaged around inside, and pulled out something triumphantly, carrying it back to her daughter. "Take them this." She held something wrapped in hencha leaves.

Jas took it and carefully unwrapped it. Inside was a single smooth black stone, about the width of her palm. "What is it?"

Lyn'Aya shook her head. "*He* would never tell me. But he said it had great value." She held it out to Jas. "Give it to them in exchange for the medicine."

Jas took it and hugged her mother. "I will." She tucked it into her pocket. "We'll leave in the morning, when Torry comes back after dropping off the harvesters. I've asked Ras'Ela to keep an eye on the cottage while I'm gone."

"That old shrew?" Her mother spit in the direction of the fire. "Half the pottery will be gone when we get home."

"Mamma!" The two older women had a bit of a love-hate relationship. Jas wondered if Ras'Ela knew about her father. "She's a *friend* and she'll make sure it doesn't burn down while we're gone."

"I'm not up to traveling." Lyn'Aya wouldn't meet her daughter's gaze.

"It's just a flitter hop. We can stay with the Sisters in Gullytown." The Sisters of the Cross were always willing to take in poor visitors for a night or two.

Lyn'Aya took a deep breath. When she looked up, her mouth was twisted like she had been chewing on a bitter bacca root. "Very well."

Jas kissed her on the cheek. "I'm tired, Mamma. I'm going to clean up a bit, and then we can get to bed." She wanted to wash off the sweet tang of the hencha and get a good night's sleep before the journey.

The trip would be hard on them both. But if there was a chance her mother could be healed…

"I… I love you, Jasinaya."

The private form of her name surprised Jas. Her mother rarely showed her such open affection. "Love you too, mamma."

TO GULLYTOWN

Sera stared at her rigged contraption. She had tied most of the plas crates to pallets on the sled rails, which were normally used to offload cargo at the end of the journey. She had primed the unloader and remapped control up to the bridge console.

She would be able to fire them off one at a time, each imparting a little reverse velocity to the ship. It was an inelegant solution, a blunt means to accomplish the desired end, but it *should* slow down the Spin Diver's headlong pace. After that, she hoped to compensate for the rest with the ship's jets.

Let it be enough.

She knelt next to the last pallet, resting a hand on the wrapped blanket she'd pulled out of the ship's stores.

"Tavi… I wish you were here with me. We were supposed to do this together." There were so many things she wanted to say but so little time.

Retrieving her wife's body from the cracked sleep pod had been the most painful thing she had ever done. The smell of decay still lingered in her nostrils.

The shrunken corpse looked nothing like the vibrant, alive woman she'd hoped to spend the rest of her life with.

Sera closed her eyes and tried to remember Tavi's beautiful smile. "You'll always be young to me." Like the first time they'd met, crossing the bridge over the Seine on a cloudy winter day in the rain.

They'd both run under a flit stop umbrella, laughing with their teeth chattering, and had spent the next half hour sharing tales of their travels.

Tavi would be happy *out there*, roaming the stars, far away from the burn-slums of Chicago where she'd been born. *Free at last.* Sera kissed her fingers and touched the blanket where it wrapped around Tavi's skull. *Goodbye, my love.*

With a sigh, she pushed down the gut-wrenching sob that threatened to break her composure. Instead, she got up and climbed the ladder to the crew level, sealing off the cargo hold behind her. If only it were so easy to seal off her regret.

They had hoped to trade those goods for asylum, for a chance to stay on Tharassas. Now she would arrive at the human colony with nothing. Well, nothing but the ship itself…

Tavi's voice sounded inside her head. *Not nothing. You have your life.* Somehow it didn't sound bitter.

Sera sank into the captain's chair. "Spin, prepare to launch first cargo package. On my count."

"Understood."

"Fire in three, two, one…"

JAS STOOD ON A WIDE PLAIN, *blades of red grass waving under the breeze that blew from somewhere distant, lifting her hair and reaching its cold fingers through her shirt.*

The wind whispered to her, carrying words she couldn't understand. She strained to hear them, but the meaning eluded her.

She could feel… something. A pressure in the back of her skull.

That whispering wind inside her own head. A rising tide inside her that threatened to wash her away.

A sharp pain in her stomach brought her gaze downward. She was swollen like a puffer hen, her belly stretched out past her slender hips.

The pain increased, and she screamed as her stomach split apart and something twisted and purple reached out of her belly, questing for the open air…

JAS AWOKE in a pool of sweat. Her hands went to her stomach, which was its usual size and most certainly unruptured. *That was odd.*

Most of her dreams were of the more mundane variety—things she'd forgotten to do the last day. Working in the plantation fields. Seeing how her life could have been different. But this…

She got up and put the nightmare out of her head. She had things to do before they left for Gullytown. She set about getting ready for the journey.

Jas packed a few belongings in a small sack. She took out the angel stone her mother had given her and stared at it, turning it over and over in her hands. *What are you?* With a shrug, she deposited it in one of her pockets.

When Lyn'Aya awoke a little later, Jas bundled her mother up in all the clothes she owned, determined to keep her warm for the journey.

Sunlight filtered through the grease-paper windows, spraying a dappled pattern across the room.

Jas had reheated the remains of the soup from the night before. They sat together and sipped it in silence until it was gone.

Her mother reached out a gnarled, almost translucent hand to touch her face. "Jasinaya… you know I'm dying."

Jas frowned. "Don't say that." Her mother's recent fatalistic streak annoyed Jas. She gathered the bowls and stood, and her mother's hand fell back to the cushion.

"I just want you to be ready. *I* am." She curled her hands together in her lap, wrapping them inside her gray homespun blanket. "I have done all the things I wanted to do in my life, including having you. I'm ready to go."

Jas rinsed out the bowls and dried them with an old cloth, a piece of one of her childhood shirts that had been repurposed, as with so many things in their humble home. "Well, *I'm not*. We're taking you to Gullytown to make you better and that's that." She threw the waste water on the fire, dousing it, and rummaged through the ashes with the poker to make sure there were no live coals.

Lyn'Aya sighed. "You always were stubborn."

"Like mother, like daughter." Jas laughed. "Come on, *old woman*." She said it affectionately, kissing her mother on the cheek.

Torry would be back any moment from his plantation run, and he wouldn't wait long. He had a job to do, too. It was only because of her long relationship with him—and the way she had flirted with him, never letting him get *too* close —that he was willing to take them at all. "We've a flitter to catch."

She led her mother out of the house and they made their way down the hillside to the green square of the flitter pad.

Corinth was quiet, with most of its able-bodied folk already at work in the hencha fields in the plantations below. Patches of fog clung to the valley floor and gully birds rode the winds up from the bay, looking for prey.

Jas paid them no mind. Her mind was elsewhere, imagining the angels—what would their ship look like? Would they be strange to her? What wonders would they bring this time?

Torry was right on time, the flitter dropping out of the sky with its sparkling wings aflutter.

Jas waved at him, hoping he didn't expect too much of a *favor* in return. She walked a fine line there.

Lyn'Aya stared at the flitter from amongst the fabric that was gathered around her face, looking like a mudmole in its hole. She looked away, shaking her head. Her face was white.

"What's wrong, mamma?"

"I don't like it. In my day we rode urses when we had to go somewhere."

Jas shook her head. "Mamma, it's perfectly safe. I ride in one every day to go to work." The flitters, along with parts to repair them, had come in with the previous Run. "Besides, if we went on urseback, we'd miss Market Day."

Lyn'Aya frowned.

Torry leaned out of the window, a welcoming grin on his face. "Hello, ma'am. Happy to have you two come aboard."

"You're not *afraid*, are you?" Jas knew all of her mother's buttons and wasn't above pushing one of them when the situation warranted.

"Afraid? No." Lyn'Aya huffed. "Just… a little concerned. For *your* safety, of course. Help your mother up into this infernal thing."

Jas grinned and boosted Lyn'Aya into the craft. "Here you go."

Soon they were both situated—Lyn'Aya in the back and Jas in the front next to Torry—and the flitter leapt into the green sky. Corinth grew rapidly smaller below as they passed over the hills and into the valley of the Heartland.

Along the southern ridgeline, little villages like hers were scattered here and there, tiny circles of homes at the base of the Tartan Hills.

On the northern side of the valley, where the Heaven's Reach mountain peaks were tall enough to still have some snow at this time of year, the great mansions of the plantation owners shone white in the late morning sun.

"I've never sat with the pilot before." Jas peered out of the clear window at the terrain below. They were passing over the first of the hencha fields and Jas could almost feel their curious thoughts.

Everyone knew they communicated amongst themselves, but no one knew how. Only a few, like her, could actually hear them.

She'd mentioned it once to Jemmy—he'd told her she was crazy.

"It gets old. All the fields look the same." Torry steered the flitter to the left and set a course toward Gullytown.

Jas shook her head. "No, they don't. The colors are different. Look—the ones in this field are a little more red. And that one over there—look how the plants are all moving. Something has them riled." She could feel the agitation in the plants below, a pressure at the back of her skull like she had felt in her dream, as if they missed her.

She laughed and shook her head. *Silly woman.*

"Maybe so. I've seen enough strange things to make me believe almost anything." He adjusted their course. "You sure it's safe for you in Gullytown?"

She turned to stare at him. "Why wouldn't it be?" She forgot that she was different, sometimes.

"There are a lot of rumors. That this ship is bringing some kind of plague. Or that it's come to destroy Gullytown, so the Earthers can take over everything."

"That's ridiculous. How would they do that? It takes twenty-five years just to get here."

"People believe what they want to." He shrugged.

She snorted. "That's true enough. You don't believe it, do you?"

"Not really." He slipped a hand absently to her knee.

She politely shifted it back. She had no interest in Mas Torry'Ost. Or *any* man. "Thank you for the ride, it's really sweet of you." She did feel a little guilty for all the flirting.

Use whatever tool's at hand. It was one of her mother's old sayings.

"Mamma, you okay back there?"

Lyn'Aya answered with a hearty snore. So much for her fear of flying.

Jas chuckled under her breath. "How long until we reach Gullytown?"

"An hour, maybe a little less." Torry stared straight ahead, pointedly not looking at her.

I embarrassed him. "I'm sorry, Torry. That was rude of me. You're very kind to do this for me."

He blushed and glanced at her. "You don't *really* like me, do you?"

She sighed. "No. Not like that."

"I thought it was too good to be true. You… you're so pretty. What does a guy like me have to offer?"

She shook her head. "It's not that."

"Then what am I missing?" He looked deflated.

She debated whether or not to be square with him. "Well… breasts, for starters."

He stared at her for a moment, then burst out laughing.

"What?" She glared at him.

"It's just… all this time I thought you *liked* me, and then I thought there was something wrong with me. But now… green skies and goose eggs, I'm an idiot."

"I'm sorry—"

"No, I get it. The world is what it is." He stared out the window in silence for a long moment. "I'm glad you told me."

That surprised her. She didn't share her personal business with many others. "You're not mad?"

He shook his head. "Just a little disappointed. But I'll live."

This time she put her hand on *his* knee. "Thank you, Torry."

He grinned. "Don't mention it."

FREEFALL

S era fought with the controls of the damaged starship. The *Spin Diver* bucked as it hit Tharassas' atmosphere, waves of heat distorting the view. Her namesake spin was off, causing the ship to wobble and corkscrew, deflecting the heat of entry unevenly.

Sera thanked God for all her months of training as the rattling of the ship made her teeth chatter. The whole craft shook and Sera feared it would break into pieces. "Spin, a little help?"

"I can fire the thrusters to reduce the eccentricity of the ship's current entry angle."

"Do it!"

"There may not be enough fuel left for a safe landing."

"If we don't get this fall under control, there won't *be* a landing." The small bridge was getting warm and sweat beaded her brow. She wiped it off with the back of her sleeve. "Cut it as close as you can."

"Understood. We're getting a request from ground control."

Sera snorted. This place saw a starship once in a generation. "Ground control" was likely an old comm set in a dusty room of whatever passed for the capital city. Bunch of mud huts, most likely. "Put them through."

"Approaching Earthship." The voice had a strange accent, though it spoke recognizable English. There was a lilt to it… something like the old British English back on Earth. "This is Dayin in Gullytown."

She growled. "Earth is dead."

"Earth is…?"

"Dead. War. Plagues. You name it." She had no patience for this.

"Okay…" Clearly the poor guy didn't know how to process that. "You're approaching us at high velocity. Are you in distress?"

"Sorry, Dayin. The ship has some damage." That was an understatement. "Suggest clearing the landing field to a radius of two kilometers."

"Two kilometers?" He sounded incredulous. "Mas, you were right. It's coming right down on top of us." That last sounded fainter, as if he was covering the comm.

"What?" She didn't need this right now.

"Are you coming destroy us?" That was directed at her.

Sera grunted. "Not intentionally. Just get everyone as far away from the landing field as you can." The ship's thrusters fired, then fired again.

"Affirmative." Dayin didn't sound like he believed her. "See you on the ground."

Fucking backwater world. "Sorry. Can't talk. See you soon." *Or not.*

It was scalding now in the small cabin. She unzipped her top, thankful for the small bit of relief.

This ended one of three ways.

A safe landing in… what was it called? Gullyport?

A hard landing in an unpopulated area.

Or a crash in the middle of this backwater civilization and innocent civilian deaths.

She planned to avoid option three at all costs.

The thrusters fired again and the bucking finally stopped. The ship settled into spin mode, and the heat on the bridge began to dissipate.

Spin's voice broke the sudden quiet. "Sera, are you okay? Your heart rate is elevated."

"Thanks, Spin. I'm good now." *From understatement to overstatement.* "How much fuel do we have left?"

"Too little for a safe landing."

"Shit." The ground below was flying up at them. She had no time.

"Get me to the edge of the landing zone, as far away from the city as you can manage."

"There's still not enough fuel for a safe—"

"Just get me there. We'll burn what we have, and then divert all of our shield power to the underside of the ship five seconds before impact. Is that clear?"

"Understood."

Was it her imagination, or was there a bit of sadness in the ship's voice? "You okay, Spin?"

There was a long, uncharacteristic pause. "I'm not going to survive this, am I?"

Sera bit her lip, hard. "I... I don't think so. I'm sorry, Spin."

An extra second of quiet accentuated the reply. "I will do all I can to save you." A pause. "It's been a hell of a ride."

Sera blinked. she hadn't expected such a *human* response from the ship's computer. "Spin—"

The AI cut her off. "Twenty seconds to impact." One of the ship's side thrusters fired and Sera fired the main rockets beneath the ship.

Below, the city, a strange collection of populated ridge lines, was expanding far too quickly as Sera rode a column of fire down toward the red landing field.

"Ten, nine, eight..."

Sorry Spin.

"Seven, six, five, four..."

Tavi, I love you —

The thrusters cut off and Sera was slammed against her chair.

Crash foam filled the cabin.

Spin's voice was muffled. "Three, two, one."

Sera blacked out.

"HOLY HENCHABALLS!"

Jas jerked awake in her seat, slamming against the restraint belt. "What?" She rubbed her eyes. She'd fallen asleep, lulled by the whir of the flitter blades and the singing of the hencha.

The hencha don't sing. Must have been a dream.

Jas glanced back at her mother in the back seat. She was still fast asleep.

"The ship from Earth. That must be what it is." Torry was straining at his belt, staring at the sky above. The flitter started to drift toward the ground.

"Hey, eye on the controls. You're making me nervous." Jas leaned forward, looking for whatever it was that had caught the pilot's attention.

"Holy—"

"Language, Jas."

So Lyn'Aya *was* awake, after all. "Holy damn." She ignored her mother's self-satisfied nod.

Something was coming down out of the green sky. There was flame and smoke, and then a loud rumble filled the air. She could feel the vibration in her bones.

Whatever it was, it looked like it was headed straight for the conical roofs of Gullytown.

"Something's wrong." Lyn'Aya was glued to her own window, hollow eyes fixed on the interloper like a field hawk.

"It wasn't like this last time?" Jas traced the invader's course. It was going to be close.

"No. It came down direct and proper-like. Not like this—"

Jas frowned "Could you see it from Corinth?"

"I wasn't in Corinth yet."

Jas turned to look at her. "What?".

"It's gonna hit the city." Torry's face was white.

She tore her eyes away from Lyn'Aya and watched the ship plummet.

They were drawing close to Gullytown. She could see the end of the hencha fields, the red grass of the landing field, and just beyond it the first of the ridges and gullies that gave the city its name.

Gullytown was built along the tops of granite spines that had been flattened to accommodate human inhabitation, and white bridges connected one of them to another over the deep gullies the Elsp River had carved out from the seafront bluffs over untold millennia. "Your family's down there?"

He nodded. "My ex-wife and our daughter live on Raven Spine."

"Look!" The ship was miraculously shifting course, moving away from the city. The roar in Jas' ears was continuous and deafening as the ship plummeted toward the ground.

"Someone must be steering it. As much as they can." Sweat beaded the pilot's forehead, but he was calmer. "Oh, to fly one of those beauties…"

"She's bringing it down on the edge of the landing field."

"She?"

Jas stared at him. "Can't a woman be a Runner?"

"I suppose so. But they usually aren't. The last time—"

The descending starship exploded in flames.

Or at least that's how it seemed to Jas.

Then she saw that the fire was shooting out of the bottom of the craft, slowing its descent. They were close enough now that she could feel the heat of it on her face.

It wasn't going to be enough.

The ship hurtled toward the grassy landing field at about a third of the speed it had gone before.

Then, just before it hit, a bright blue glow surrounded its base, extinguishing the flame.

The ship slammed into the ground, throwing up a cloud of red grass, dirt and smoke. Then it was quiet, the sudden, uneasy silence that only exists after an ear-splitting sound.

Jas stared at the broken craft. There was another human being on that ship, someone with blood like hers in their veins, with a heart that beat just like hers.

Jas made up her mind. "Get me down there."

Torry stared at her. "Have you gone henchwine mad?"

She shook her head. "*Someone* steered that ship away from the city at the last minute. If they're still alive, they may be injured or unable to get out."

"The city guard will take care of it—"

"Look around! All traffic is grounded. There *is* no one else." Jas challenged him to deny her.

He held her gaze for a second or two, then nodded. "Crap, I'm gonna regret this—"

"Language!" Lyn'Aya seemed to care more about policing their conversation than the impending danger.

"Damn. I'm gonna regret this. I'll drop you as close as I can, then I'm pulling out."

"Deal." Jas reached back and squeezed her mother's hand, expecting an argument. "Mamma, I gotta do this—"

Her mother squeezed back with surprising strength and nodded. "Go."

The flitter swooped in under the plume of black smoke and managed a nimble landing about fifty meters from the downed ship.

"Love you, mamma." Jas swung the flitter door open, slipped out to the ground and ran.

Sera awoke, vaguely aware of a dim red light flashing in the darkness. Her head pounded and she couldn't hear a thing. *Where am I?*

Her left leg ached.

She lifted her head. She was covered with something sticky. *Crash foam.*

It all came back to her. The destruction of the Earth. The long flight. The awakening and Tavi.

The crash.

In the flashing crimson light, she could just make out her legs. The left one was stained with something dark and wet.

She reached out and touched it, bringing her fingers to her nose.

They had the tangy smell of blood, mixed with the antiseptic smell of the decaying foam.

She struggled to get up and immediately doubled over in pain as she put pressure on her injured leg. More blood spurted out of the cut.

Seven light years from Earth and I'm gonna die planet-side from something as stupid as simple blood loss.

She lay still until the pain lessened. Then she looked up at what was left of the bridge's control console. At that flashing red light.

Imminent Destruction.

Oh fuck. The ship's core had been damaged in the crash. If she didn't get out quickly, she'd leave nothing but a crater to be remembered by. "Spin!"

No response. She felt a moment's regret for the noble AI. Then she levered herself up, ignoring the pain as best as she could.

She put a little weight on her leg again and screamed in pain. She fell back to the sticky metal floor of the bridge.

"Tavi! Tavi help me!" It came out as more of an anguished gurgle than a voice. *Tavi's gone. And soon I will be too.*

Sera lay there on the floor and a curious sense of peace came over her. There was nothing else she could do. She had put up a fight, had given it all she had, and now fate was taking her down.

Sera wasn't religious, but for a moment she wondered if maybe, just maybe, Tavi was waiting for her out there somewhere. Beyond all of *this*.

She closed her eyes, her cheek pressed against the warm sticky floor, and prayed for someone to come. Or for a quick death.

JAS PEERED through the open hatchway of the broken ship.

Something or someone had opened it. A blaring noise issued from inside. It was like staring into the guts of some fell metal beast out of her worst nightmares.

A blue liquid leaked out of the ship onto the grass, filled with bubbles.

She touched it. It was warm but didn't burn her hands. It smelled... salty? Sharp? Not like anything else she knew.

Behind the ship, from one edge of the horizon to the other, the hencha plants swayed and sang.

Jas shook her head, dispelling the hallucination. *No time to waste.* She climbed up into the ship, her work boots finding purchase on the bumpy metallic floor.

The hallway sat at a strange angle. She struggled to navigate it, checking the rooms off to each side for passengers.

Flashing red lights ahead illuminated her way.

At the end of the hall, there was a ladder on one side,

leading down to who-knew-where, and a partially-open doorway ahead of her.

Undecided, she was about to try the ladder when she heard a crash in the room ahead. Someone—or something—was in there.

She stuffed down her fear and pushed on one side of the door, managing to open it a few centimeters more.

It wasn't enough.

"Anyone in there?"

"Yes. Help me!" A woman's voice. At least, it *sounded* feminine.

"Hold on!" Back in one of the rooms, she'd seen a broken pipe. It would have to do.

Jas retraced her steps and found the length of metal. It took a bit of wrenching to get it off the wall, but Jas was strong, and soon she had a lever to help her open the door.

She inserted it in-between the door and the frame and managed to force it open half a meter.

She covered her ears. The noise was really loud inside.

There was a figure stretched out on the floor, covered in the blue fluid. Probably the pilot.

Jas hurried over to her, kneeling in the sticky substance. She touched the woman's neck and was relieved to feel that her pulse was strong.

The pilot moaned.

"Are you okay?" Jas had to shout over the din.

"Yes."

"Are there any others?"

The pilot shook her head. "Just me."

That was strange. Her mother had told her that these ships usually carried a full crew—four or six people, at least.

There was no time to worry about it now. "Are you injured?"

"My leg. Cut. Ship's about to blow."

Jas shivered. *That* didn't sound good. "Okay, I'm going to help you get up. Put your arm around me."

She managed to lever the woman up to put an arm under her shoulder. It was tricky with the strange angle of the floor, but soon they were standing.

Every time the pilot put weight on her leg, she whimpered. "It fucking hurts."

Mamma would be annoyed by such rank language. Jas grinned. "Come on. You can hop on your good leg."

They maneuvered their way out of the room and down the hall toward the exit. An acrid black smoke was filling the ship. Jas held her breath and closed her eyes to slits.

The alarm shut off, leaving them in sudden silence. It was almost worse than the awful sound—things were going downhill quickly.

They reached the exit. "Here, lean against the wall."

The woman did as she was told, wincing at the pain, and Jas jumped down to the ground. She held out her arms like her mother used to do for her. "Come on. Jump."

The woman glanced over her shoulder, and when she looked back, her cheeks were streaked with tears.

She jumped. Her weight knocked Jas back onto the ground.

Jas struggled to get up, dusting off the red dirt, and helped the pilot to her feet. "I'm Jas.

"Sera."

"Nice to meet you. Now come on. Let's go!" They climbed out of the crater that surrounded the ship and stumbled together across the field, struggling to get as far away from the ship as they could.

Jas had just become aware of the crowd gathered a couple hundred meters ahead when a *roar* from behind her consumed her senses and sent her flying once more onto the grassy earth.

GROUNDED

Sera sat up, rubbing her temples. She looked around, confused, trying to get her bearings.

Just moments before, she'd been face-down in a puddle of melted crash foam, waiting for the world to end. Now she was sitting on a grassy field under a green sky, only the grass was a weird red, almost purple at the edges of the blades.

Her leg still throbbed, but the worst of the bleeding had stopped.

There had been a woman in blue. Like the Virgin Mary. *That wasn't my imagination, was it?*

She looked around and spotted her savior.

She looked less angelic now, sprawled out awkwardly on the grass about two meters from Sera, her head turned away. She was dressed in a blue shirt and skirt, but the outfit looked more practical than pretty. She had dark hair, like Tavi.

Sera's hearing was slowly returning.

White birds circled lazily overhead. She squinted at them —bird *equivalents* anyway. Their wings were... wrong. Bent forward instead of backward, like terrestrial birds.

Sera hoped they weren't the local version of vultures.

Gritting her teeth, she dragged herself across the grass toward the woman, hoping she was still alive.

Jas. Had she dreamed that part? "Jas! Are you okay?"

Jas grunted.

Sera shook her shoulder gently. "You okay?"

Jas pushed herself up on her elbows. "I think so." Her accent was strange, like something between British English and Italian. "You?" Her skin was tanned. She was beautiful.

"Bad cut on my leg. But otherwise I seem to be. You have medics here?"

Jas stared at her.

"Doctors?"

"Ah yes. Are you rich?"

"What?"

Jas smiled disarmingly. "Your hands. They aren't rough and calloused." She held up her own. They were the hands of someone who did honest work.

Sera blushed. "No. Just don't do much manual labor." She and Tavi had worked the local Earth-to-Luna Run for years before scoring this gig, and flying a spacecraft was a lot less manually intensive than… well, probably anything on Tharassas.

Tavi. Pain clenched her gut. "Didn't get out much."

Jas was staring at something over Sera's shoulder. "Looks like we're about to have company."

Sera turned, wincing at the pain in her leg.

A small delegation was approaching them, all blond men. Behind that group, a large crowd had gathered along the edge of the wide landing field. Almost every one of them was blond too, and they looked angry.

"Go home!" one of women in the crowd shouted. Soon the rest took up the chant.

"Aliens go home! Aliens go home!"

Aliens? They must think that Jas was from the ship too.

The leader of the delegation, a short man with *very* white

skin, looked grim as he bore down on them, and the others carried *things* that looked like medieval spears, topped with wickedly sharp blades.

That can't be good.

∽

JAS STARED at the approaching delegation. They looked angry.

She put on an urgent look and waved at them. "Oh, thank the hencha you're here. Did you bring a doctor? She needs help!" She ignored the idiots jeering at the edge of the field.

The man leading the party stopped and stared at her and turned to whisper something to a taller man dressed in a red jamja marking him as one of the clerical class.

He looked unhappy at having been dragged out into the open wilds. Such as they were.

Jas frowned. Sera was hurt. They should be running to help her.

"I'm going to need you to step aside, Mim…"

"Mim Aya. Jas'Aya. And you are?" She got up and brushed off the dirt and blades of grass from her skirt. The fall had left red stains from the grass across the lower end of it. She sighed—those were going to be hard to get out.

"Mas Errol. Head of security for the Heartland Council."

"Mas Errol." She nodded at him. "Can I ask why you need me out of the way?" This didn't smell right. She looked up at the green sky, wondering where Torry had gone with her mother. *Might be handy to have a flitter ride, right about now.*

"As I said, Mim Aya, I need you to step aside. We have to take care of this problem before it escalates."

She really didn't like the sound of that. "This *problem*?" She put her hands on her hips. "By *problem*, do you mean Mim…" She glanced back at Sera. "What's your surname?"

Sera was watching the whole thing with wide eyes. "Collins."

Strange name. "Mim Collins?"

The man looked flustered. "I'm afraid so. The council sent me to… to deal with… Mim Collins. You are the pilot of that ship?" He pointed at the still-smoking wreckage at the edge of the landing field. "One of the runners?"

"Yes."

"Where are the others?"

A pained look crossed Sera's face. "All dead. I'm the only survivor."

Mas Errol looked relieved. He turned to his colleagues for support. "Mim Collins told our flight control officer that the Earth is dead, that there was some sort of plague. She has admitted to trying to destroy Gullytown with her…" he looked over at the broken ship. "Weapon."

Jas snorted. "Weapon? That's a ship, not a weapon."

"Nevertheless. We also suspect Mim Collins may be carrying a contagion, based on her own statements to our ground controller."

Jas shot Sera a look. "Did you mention something about a contagion?"

The pilot nodded miserably. "There were plagues, back on Earth. Human-made plagues. But I'm not sick—"

"So either she's lying," and he paused as if it were patently unbelievable, "or she might have brought whatever it was that destroyed the Earth here with her."

Sera snorted. "Where? In my pockets?"

Mim Errol's gaze hardened. "We're not savages, Mim Collins. We know about germs and the genetic sciences."

Jas signaled to Sera to be quiet. "I assume by 'take care of,' you mean 'perform a thorough investigation, and if punishment is warranted, give her a fair trial?" She stared him down.

He stared at her, trying to speak, but nothing came out.

Behind the party, a crowd had begun to encroach on the scene, staying a few meters behind the men. They were quiet now, but the angry looks on their faces were unchanged.

Mim Errol turned away first. "Of course."

Out loud to the crowd, Jas said "I found this woman. Under Heartland law, I claim Squatter's Rights over Mim Collins and all her property."

There was an audible gasp from the crowd.

Undaunted, Jas pushed ahead. "Any claims over her or against her are now to be channeled through me. Am I understood?"

Her heart was racing. Squatter's rights had been in wide use a century before, when the Valley was still half empty. Her mother had taught her all about them. But to her knowledge they had never been used in quite this way. It was a gamble, and one which very well might end up with her dead.

Still, she couldn't just stand by and do nothing while they killed the runner in front of her.

Nothing ventured…

The group of men conferred for a moment. At last, the short one turned back to her. "We accept your terms. But you will be incarcerated with Mim Collins until this matter can be worked out." He wrung his hands. "You understand our need for caution, I'm sure. You might have been exposed to an unknown pathogen."

Sera snorted. "I've had all my shots."

Jas ignored her. "I accept your terms. Now can someone get a stretcher to carry my property? She's not going to carry herself."

Saying Sera belonged to her sounded weird, even to Jas, but she had to keep up her end of the game.

"Property? I'm not—"

"Play along," Jas whispered as she knelt next to Sera to check her leg. It was still oozing blood, but much more slowly than before. "These men were sent here to kill you."

Sera's eyes went wide.

"You and I should be kept together while we prepare our defense with an advocate. Say nothing else now. We'll talk more when we're alone together. Do you understand?"

Sera's eyes widened, but she nodded. "I understand."

In minutes two men arrived carrying a stretcher. They had cloth masks around their faces and leather gloves on their hands. They lifted Sera gently into the stretcher and carried her back toward the city.

Jas followed, giving Mas Errol a dirty look.

He glared back at her.

Jas hoped she was doing the right thing. It had all happened so quickly, and she hadn't had time to think it through.

Her whole reason for coming here, for taking such a risk, was to get medicine for her mother. A glance back at the smoking ruins of the starship told her that wasn't going to happen.

She fervently wished her mother was there to hold her hand, to share her sage wisdom with her only daughter.

Lyn'Aya would have known what to do, and she would have made short work of the men sent to tackle the *problem*.

Mamma, where are you?

TRAPPED

Jas sat on the hard stone floor, staring at the thick wooden door that blocked off part of the wine cavern into a smaller room for storage.

The Heartland *colony*—she supposed they'd have to stop calling it that now that Earth was gone—lacked a formal prison. Most justice was meted out with a whip or a stay in the stocks in the public square, or both.

But the wine caverns provided a suitable place to hold her while the powers-that-be decided what to do with her.

And Sera.

If something hadn't *already* been done.

They had been separated against Jas' will. One of the guards had explained that Sera's leg needed tending, which made no sense if they really thought she might be carrying some kind of contagion. She was sure it was all a sham.

Now Sera was nowhere to be seen, and Jas' worry was getting the better of her.

Jas got up and studied the door. The hinges were on the outside, and there wasn't even a hencha leaf's breadth between the wood of the door and its frame.

It was made of thick oak boards—one of the modified

Earth trees that had managed to take root on Tharassas—and was banded in iron.

"Hello?" Her voice echoed around the small room. "Hello!" No one answered.

She paced her way around the room for the tenth or twentieth time, stopping to stare at the electric lamp that hung from the ceiling.

In that respect, the cavern was more luxurious than her own home, which was lit only by sunlight and hencha oil.

Gullytown had electric power thanks to their hydroelectric dam, built in part with supplies from Earth. They really were going to have to learn to stand up on their own.

After making the circuit, she pulled out the strange round stone her mother had given her. What good had it ended up being?

Sera had come here with nothing to trade—no exotic spices, no colorful bolts of Earth-made fabric, no replacement parts for aging machinery. No fanciful wings for a little girl to fly with.

No medicine.

She wanted to throw the stone against the wall, to smash it into a thousand pieces. Instead she slipped it back into her pocket.

She was worried about the angry mood in Gullytown. Something had folks riled up, almost as if they had been primed for Sera's arrival. She was trapped here, all alone, and somewhere out there, her mother was sick, maybe dying. Lost. Missing her.

She had probably thrown away the only job she had to come here, on the small chance that she could find a cure for whatever was killing Lyn'Aya.

And now—

Something clanked.

The lock. The door creaked open, dragging on the ground,

revealing two of the city guards. They were supporting Sera between them.

She walked with a limp. She was sweating, but otherwise appeared unharmed. She had been cleaned up and given fresh clothing not unlike Jas' own.

"What's happening? I want to see my advocate." Jas debated slipping past the black-clad guards while they were occupied, but she decided that she wouldn't get very far. She was in a cavern beneath the city, and even if she found her way out, she didn't know her way around Gullytown or anyone who lived there.

Besides, there was Sera to consider.

After they helped the runner sit on the hard floor, one of the guards, a stocky blond with a scar across his cheek, turned to her. "Your advocate will see you in the morning."

"When is that?" Jas put her hands on her hips. "It's rather hard to tell time down here."

"About seven hours from now." Then he turned to go.

Another man, wearing the green of the servant class, came in with a tray laden with food.

Jas' stomach rumbled. At least they wouldn't starve to death while they waited. "Thank you."

The man nodded and set the tray down a few feet from them. Then he backed out of the room quickly, following the guards out.

The door closed with a heavy thud.

"So this is the local prison, huh?" Sera was looking at the rough-hewn walls.

"Pretty much." Jas sat across from her and started serving the food—three-legged gully fowl and a loaf of dense bread— onto the two earthenware plates the servant had brought in. "Did they treat you well?"

"They didn't hurt me, if that's what you're asking." Sera took her share. "I was hoping for a better welcome than this."

"Then you should have brought better gifts." Jas flashed her a grin.

Sera snorted. "Touché."

"Toosh...?"

"It means 'exactly,' or 'you're right.' Kind of." She looked at the food. "Are you sure it's safe to eat?"

Jas nodded. "If they wanted to kill us, there are much easier ways."

"Makes sense." Sera sniffed at the bread and then took a cautious nibble. "Not bad."

Jas took a bite out of one of the gully fowl legs—it was delicious, spiced with something she couldn't identify. Much more than the basic salt she was allotted back home in Corinth.

She tried not to stare at Sera. The runner was beautiful—tall, thin, her skin the warm color of the earth. Darker than Jas' own lighter-but-tanned skin.

Sera caught her staring. "Never seen someone quite like me, have you?"

Jas blushed and shook her head. "My mother said she had sex with an angel, but I think he was more like me than you."

"An angel?"

"One of the runners, like you."

Sera laughed, but there was pain behind it. "Tavi, my... girlfriend—do you have those here?"

Jas nodded. Her heart started to beat a little faster. Sera was beautiful. Exotic. And she liked women. "We do."

"Tavi looked a bit like you. Stockier, but her eyes... they were brown like yours and she had dark hair." She turned away, taking a bite of her bread and staring at the door.

Jas took a deep breath. "They said... you said that the Earth was gone?"

Sera's gaze snapped back to hers. "Yeah. Might as well be. Big war between the Lagrange Nation in orbit and the Union on the surface. Pretty much wiped out both—it will be decades or centuries before anything approaching civilization springs up again there. Tavi and I, we saw it coming—"

"What happened to her?" Jas regretted it as soon as the words came out of her mouth. "I'm sorry. I shouldn't have asked—"

"It's okay." Sera chewed on a hunk of the bread. "Her sleep pod was damaged, I think. It malfunctioned. She… didn't make it."

Jas put a hand out on Sera's knee. "I'm sorry."

It was a *lot* to take in. Earth had always been more of a legend to her than a real thing. It was so far away, in both space and time. And yet, it was where humankind had been born. To learn it was no longer there… "I guess we're on our own now."

Sera nodded. "Looks like it. Mine was the last Run."

Jas sat back, pouring some water into a cup from the glass bottle the servant had brought with the meal.

The colony was mostly self-sufficient, but some things couldn't be made here. Not yet. Flitter parts. Power sources. Medicines. They were reliant on a planet that no longer existed.

"Why were you there?" Sera was staring at her fingernails.

Jas snapped back to the present. "What?"

"On the landing field. You saved me before the ship blew." Her green eyes looked back at Jas over the edge of her own cup. "No one else was even close—we warned them away."

"We?"

"Me and the ship's AI… the ship computer."

"Ah." She knew about computers, though she'd never seen one. The colony had a few in the Council hall. "I was on my way to find you."

Sera's eyebrow raised. "Really?"

"Well, Not *you* in particular. But the ship. The angels."

The edge of Sera's lips quirked up. "You know we're not really angels."

It was Jas' turn to laugh. "Yeah, guess that's obvious now. No wings."

Sera looked over her shoulder. "Must have left them on the ship."

Jas grinned. She liked this angel—this runner. This person. "My mother's sick. I wanted to get medicine to make her better." Said out loud, it sounded stupid. "I'm sorry—you probably would have had more important things to do."

This time it was Sera who put a hand on her knee. "I wish I could have helped her. And thank you."

Jas frowned. "For what? Getting you thrown in jail?"

"For saving my life."

"Oh, that." It had simply seemed necessary at the time.

"What were you going to trade for it?"

"What?" *That* got Jas' ire up. "You think that just because I'm a simple field hand, I don't have anything worth trading?"

Sera put up her hands. "Sorry, didn't mean it as an insult. I was just curious." Her eyes searched Jas'.

"Oh. Sorry." She pulled the package her mother had given her out of her pocket. She unwrapped the leaves. "I don't know what this is. But she said her angel, her human—her runner gave it to her and told her it was valuable."

Sera took it and grinned. "She was right. It's an older model, but if it still works... may I?"

Jas shrugged.

Sera felt around the edge of the thing. "Here it is." She pushed something, and a ring of blue light surrounded the stone.

"Run diagnostic?" A deep, professional-sounding voice emanated from the previously silent stone.

Jas scrambled backward. "What in the holy hencha was that?"

Sera laughed. "It's okay. It's just a device. A tool." To the stone, she said "Yes." She held it out in front of her and the blue light expanded to bathe her body.

In that instant Jas understood how very far away the Earth had been from Tharassas—both in distance and technological capability. It was like watching someone perform magic.

The light went off. "Subject has a laceration on the left leg and a slight calcium deficiency. Otherwise the subject is in good health. Repair laceration?"

"No, thank you."

"Shutting down." The stone went dark.

"What. Was. That?" Jas was aware that her mouth hung open like a child's.

"It's a DNH… a diagnostics and healing device. This is a field model with fairly limited capabilities—the kind many ships carry in their emergency kits." She stared at Jas. "Whoever gave this to your mother must have really loved her. He took a great risk removing it from the ship and broke half a dozen LPC regs."

"LPC?"

"Local Population Contact regulations. They're there to prevent us from contaminating the local culture." She frowned. "Not that it matters anymore."

"So it's like a doctor?" Jas looked at the stone with newfound respect. "Could it heal my mother?"

"I don't know. It's not very sophisticated. But it might tell you what's wrong with her."

Jas snorted. *Not very sophisticated.* It was a magic box that *talked.* She threw her arms around Sera. "Thank you!" She squeezed the woman tightly.

As she became aware of the close proximity of Sera's skin, her face got hot. *It's been too long.* Her last fling had ended two years before, when Zay'Ina had moved away with her family.

"Hey, watch the leg!"

Jas backed away carefully. "Are you okay?"

"Think so. They cleaned it up really well. And Crash Foam *is* antiseptic."

Jas frowned.

"Means it kills germs."

"Ah." More magic.

"If we get out of here, I'll help you try to figure out what's wrong with your mother."

"Thank you." Jas felt hopeful for the first time in a year—unrealistic, irrational hope, but hope nonetheless. Maybe their advocate would be able to arrange a visit with her mother. Then, even if the worst happened…

Sera was staring at her.

"Sorry, I was just thinking about my mother."

"I thought so. Mine died five years before the war."

Jas stared at her, unable to comprehend the scope of Sera's loss. Her whole world was gone—everything and everyone she had ever known. "We should try to get some rest. Tomorrow the advocate will meet with us."

"Advocate… is that like a lawyer?"

"He'll be our representative before the Council." She hoped they would be given time to prepare a defense.

Sera nodded. "Close enough." She looked around. "No beds, huh?"

Jas shook her head. "I mean, yes, we have them. But not here." She settled in against the rock wall, trying to find a comfortable position.

Sera did the same.

Jas closed her eyes. So many strange and amazing things had happened since yesterday—the flitter ride, the ship's arrival, the arrest—she was exhausted just thinking about them.

In moments she was fast-asleep.

DREAMS

Sera lay against the cool, hard stone, trying to ignore the painful throbbing in her leg.

The DNH could have provided a measure of relief with some analgesics—even helped along the healing process. But it had a limited amount of power, especially when it hadn't been charged for several decades. The x-cores in small electronics like that were rated for fifteen or twenty years—it was a minor miracle that it was still running after all this time.

Besides, Jas' mother needed it more.

The other woman's breathing slowed to an even in and out that Sera found soothing. She used to watch Tavi when she slept, as her wife purred like a kitten.

This was a strange world. The sky was the wrong color. So were the plants, and almost everyone was blond. The castes seemed to be well defined by the color of clothing each person wore, and she wondered what happened to anyone who tried to step out of them.

It was so different from the free-wheeling multi-cultur-alism of Earth, where the only thing everyone had in common was that they were all different. Different colors, different genders (or combinations or lack thereof), even different body types, with many opting for more animal forms or cyborg enhancements.

Sera closed her eyes, wishing she were home in her own bed with Tavi at her side. They had sacrificed everything to win this Run, to escape a collapsing Earth. Now she was here at last, and she was all alone.

Maybe it's not such a bad thing if they decide to kill me. Sera wasn't a religious person, but who knew what strange secrets the universe held? Maybe they had their own Heaven here on Tharassas, and Tavi was in some Great Beyond, waiting for her with that lopsided smile. *Tavi, are you out there?*

There was no response.

So much lost. So many things she'd left behind.

Eventually, she fell into a troubled sleep, interrupted by memories of Tavi, her face broken into pieces like a nightmare Picasso version of herself.

JAS DREAMED TOO.

Strange voices whispered all around her, and hands like fronds massaged her skin, holding her in a strange embrace.

Her mother was there. She was younger, though, and there was someone else too. A man.

She smelled the freshly turned earth, heard the rustle of hencha leaves all around her.

Something spoke her name, and the pressure built up in the back of her head like water behind a dam, until she thought her skull would burst.

Jas awoke in a cold sweat. She wiped her brow with the back of her arm and looked around. Sera lay on the ground next to her, her head on her arm.

Someone was turning a key in the door lock.

She sat up, rubbing her eyes. "Sera!" She reached over and

shook the other woman's foot. "Wake up! I think the advocate is here."

"What?" Sera's head snapped up. She rubbed her neck. "I wish you people had beds in your prisons, like civilized folk."

Jas shook her head. "Shhhh. The advocate is here," Jas repeated. "No joking. Follow my lead." Jas knew her rights. Lyn'Aya had drilled them into her.

The door swung open, and Jas squinted into the bright light from the main cavern outside.

Mas Errol, the head of security who had threatened them the day before, stepped into the cavern. He was alone save for the two guards carrying shock-sticks.

Jas frowned. "Where's my advocate?"

"Hello, Mim Aya. The Council has designated me in that role. Please follow me."

Jas stared at him. "I don't understand…"

He looked at her like she was a recalcitrant child. "It means that they have decided that I am to be your advocate."

She shook her head. "This isn't right. I demand another advocate."

Mas Errol shook his head. "I'm sorry. You *are* guaranteed an advocate. But the law states very clearly that you don't get to choose them yourself. Or dispute the choice of the Council." He smiled, but it was cold. "I promise to be fair and impartial."

Sera grunted. "That seems unlikely."

"Nevertheless. These guards are going to secure you. Then I ask that you follow me."

The two guards tied her arms behind her back with hencha rope. Then they helped Sera up and tied hers too.

Sera shot a quizzical glance at Jas.

Jas shook her head. "Go along," she mouthed.

Sera nodded.

Jas' fear was growing, but she had to trust in the Law.

The guards nudged the two of them along through the open door. Sera limped along next to her, managing well enough with her injured leg. They emerged from the room into the larger cave where the barrels of henchwine were stored—row upon row of red banded barrels stacked up to the ceiling. Likely half of the barrels had been laid down for trade with Earth, where henchwine was—or had been—very popular.

The air was crisp and humid. It was a little dank inside the cavern, permeated with the smells of wine and dust and old wood.

As a fifth-generation colonist, Earth was a distant realm to Jas, one she would never see in her lifetime. But it had always been there… even if the only way to get to it was a twenty-five-year trip.

Now that it was gone, Jas felt a strange emptiness in her chest. *How long will we survive without it?*

Soon they emerged into the sunlight, following a paved path that led up the edge of the spine to Gullytown above.

A stark black rock wall loomed over her on the left, dotted with red ferns, while far below on her right waves crashed in the inlet between the two spines of rock, sending up a salty spume that coated the rock in a thin mist.

Jas again felt the pressure in the back of her mind. It was like the start of a bad headache or a distant din of voices.

She shook her head and it retreated, but she could still sense it there, like a coiled beast waiting for release.

The conical red roofs of Gullytown crowded the top of the spine above her, sunlight trickling down between them. Gully birds cried out and swept low to check out the people who were invading their realm, their cries like the mewing of a baby.

The small party crested the spine and entered the main road that ran between the rows of houses. A crowd lined the street, many of them wearing servant green, a few of their masters wearing white. No one else was wearing blue like her.

A woman in red shook her head and spat at Jas' feet before hurriedly backing away. "Filthy harvester."

Jas turned away, shaken by the hatred on the faces all around her. *Mother, where are you?*

Their escort turned and led them down the cobblestone street. Through the gaps in the houses, Jas could see the edge of Gullytown's central spine where it dropped off to the ravine far below.

Crowds of people were streaming across the white bridges from the other spines that paralleled this one, and the people who already stood along the street craned their necks for a look at the runner and her companion.

Jas frowned. "Isn't the Council Chambers that way?" She looked over her shoulder—she could see the white domed building at the end of the street behind her.

Mas Errol's face was a stone mask. "We're not going to Council Chambers."

Jas felt a sick feeling stirring in her gut.

Some in the crowd were openly jeering them now and the people drew away from them as they passed.

"Take your germs and your dirty skin and go home."

"Why did you come here? Did you want to kill us all?"

"You sick farks!" That one was accompanied by a rock that whizzed past Jas' head close enough for her to hear it.

Jas looked ahead and her blood ran cold. They were being taken back out to the landing field.

This was starting to feel less like a trial than a public execution.

"What's happening?" Sera looked frightened, inching closer to Jas.

"I wish I knew." She wanted to take Sera's hand and squeeze it, to tell her that everything would be okay, but something was going on here that she didn't understand.

A flitter zoomed low past them and then angled toward the grassy fields ahead.

They left the last of the buildings behind and the crowd around them began to spill out of the city street. The road turned left to circle around the edge of the landing field. Off to the right, the river that had carved out the gullies that gave the town its name tumbled down into them with a continuous rushing crash.

Instead of following the road, the guards led them out into the field. The crowd followed at a distance.

A conical stack of wood rose above the plain ahead like a monument.

Jas stopped. "No. You can't." She stumbled backward, but one of the guards pressed the butt of his shock stick against her back.

It was a punishment reserved for the most heinous of criminals—those who raped children or killed another human being. Death on the pyre.

"What is it?" Sera's eyes were wide.

Mas Errol frowned. "Well, I guess this will do as well as anywhere. We've had our eyes on you for a while," he whispered to Jas. "You're too close to the hencha. Just our luck you ended up here with her."

Jas stared at him. *What about the Law?*

Mas Errol pulled out a hencha-leaf scroll and began to read aloud, raising his voice so the crowd could hear. "Seeing that the accused Mim Sera Collins has confessed to carrying a deadly infectious agent, and seeing that her companion, Mim Jas'Aya, has aided, abetted, and been in close contact with said accused, the Council hereby orders both women to be ritually burned to destroy the contagion and protect the colony."

"What in the gully hell are you talking about?" If Jas could have, she would have throttled the smug little man. She pulled at the cords that bound her wrists, but they were tied firmly behind her back. "She's not sick."

"Honest, I didn't bring anything with me." Sera looked shell-shocked at the pronouncement.

Mas Errol scowled. "Sometimes a message needs to be sent. To Earth and to more… local troublemakers."

The guards prodded them from behind with the butts of their shock sticks, making a show of being afraid to touch them.

Jas growled. The guards *knew* it was all a lie. They had shown no such reluctance to touch her and Sera when binding the hands of their captives. She was glad Lyn'Aya wasn't here. At least her mother was safe. Sick, but safe. The irony of that thought almost undid her.

She stumbled forward toward the pyre, looking back and forth for a way out of this as she and Sera were herded forward. In the distance, the hencha swayed as if they were one.

Jas felt that strange pressure in the back of her head and pushed it away once again. This was no time for nightmares —she needed to keep a clear head. But fear flooded her mind, making such clarity nearly impossible.

The flitter she had seen before slipped past them again, but this time it settled to the ground, dropping neatly between them and the pyre.

The door opened up and her mother got out, standing taller than Jas had seen her do in years. Her voice rang out clearly across the grass landing zone, hushing the crowd.

"What is the meaning of this?"

Mas Errol turned toward her, and his face went white. "What… what are you doing here, Mim Aya?"

Jas stopped in her tracks, stunned. The head of security knew her mother? And why had he used the most formal form of address with her?

"You should be ashamed of yourself, Judin Errol. You and

the rest of the council. Your father would be." She advanced on him, coughing once on her sleeve but otherwise seeming the picture of strength and health. "What, exactly, were you planning to do with my daughter?"

Mas Errol gulped. "Your... your daughter?" Something had clearly been left out of the intelligence packet.

Jas' mother reached her and hugged her. "Are you okay, Jasinaya?" she whispered into Jas' ear.

"Yes, mamma... but—"

"Shhhh. Let me take care of this." She turned back to Mas Errol. "Have these girls had a proper hearing?"

Mas Errol sputtered. "The Council felt that—"

"That they could ignore the Founding Papers?"

He looked very uncomfortable, looking to the guards for support. "Yes... no ma'am."

"Right answer."

Jas had never been prouder of her mother.

Lyn'Aya drew herself up. "Now, I fully expect that you will follow Heartland law and—"

"You have no power here anymore." The crowd parted and a tall man all dressed in white emerged. It was clear from his bearing and how those around him deferred to him that he was important. "You abdicated your position when you chose a *runner* over your own kind." He made the word drip with disgust.

He was about Lyn'Aya's age, to look at him, but Jas had no idea who he was.

"Artur. I'm so glad you are here. This man has made a real mess of things, flouting Council law and the Founding—"

Artur... Mas Vellin. "Mamma, don't..."

Mas Vellin sneered at the three of them. "This woman touched her daughter. She's probably contaminated." He turned to the crowd. "These three came here to destroy us, to ruin our way of life. This one"—he indicated Sera—"Came from Earth in a desperate attempt to take over our own world for her masters."

Jas shook her head. That didn't even make sense. But the crowd cheered and jeered, their cries rising to a fever pitch.

"And these two conspired with her to help bring us down." He raised his hands, shaking them dramatically in the air, his fair skin turning red. "Burn them. Burn them all!"

The crowd exploded into chanting. "Burn them! Burn them! Burn them!" Their faces were all as red as Mas Vellin's.

"No!" Jas threw herself in front of her mother. "Take me. Not her." The pressure was growing again inside her mind. Like the rising of a tidal wave, sweeping up everything in its path, its power fueled by the urgent weight of her fear and rage.

She shoved it aside once more, but it groaned in her head like water pushing on a dam.

The guards seized the three of them and strong-armed them all toward the pyre.

How did this happen? Jas tried to kick the guards, spat in their faces, but they pushed her and her companions unerringly forward.

The world around her spun in and out of her vision, the red grass and the green sky bleeding into one and then splitting apart again like the colors in a the kaleidoscope.

Behind them, Mas Errol raised his voice to be heard over the muttering of the crowd. "These women have been found to besshhheareggggh!"

The world around Jas slipped and blurred again, Mas Errol's words slurring into gibberish. She fought the turmoil inside her, trying to push it down again, but she couldn't hold it back anymore. The dam burst, and the wave rushed toward her.

She barely felt the touch of the guards as her hands were untied from each other and then bound to the wood of the pyre.

A sense of wild alarm drowned her and she writhed in agony as the wave crashed through her, dousing her nerves like burning hencha oil.

The world slipped and turned.

Lyn'Aya and her angel, the man from Earth, running into the hencha fields hand in hand, lying down on the rich loamy earth together, moving together in a way as old as humankind.

Jas' eyes flew open. Something was wrong with her. Very wrong.

The singing of the hencha all around them, while Lyn'Aya and Jason created a new life amongst them.

Jas panted, her brow heavy with sweat.

Her conception.

Something was coming, shifting and growing inside her, carrying her along helplessly, just as she had grown inside Lyn'Aya's belly after that fateful night.

And it wanted *out*.

FIRE

Sera was on the verge of panic.

She didn't want to die.

All this time, she'd thought she was ready. Ready to go join Tavi in whatever great beyond might await them. Ready to let go of the pain—physical and emotional—that beset her. Ready to be *done*.

But now that it was here, she wasn't ready. She didn't want to die. Not like this, on a strange planet in a whirlwind of pain and fire.

"Why are you doing this?" She stared at the guard, a woman younger than she was, dressed all in black, her blonde hair tied tightly into a top knot.

"I'm sorry. They say you're sick." Her blue eyes met Sera's.

"You *know* that's a lie."

The woman looked away, cinching the knot holding her to the pyre. "I'm so sorry. They said… they said you were all traitors. I don't think you are. But I can't…" Her voice cracked. "I just can't. I have a family. I'm so sorry."

Jas' mother was being tied to the pyre on Sera's left. "I'm sorry too, dear. This shouldn't be happening."

Sera started shaking. "I don't want to die. I don't want to die!"

The guard stepped away, her face down, unable to meet Sera's gaze.

"I know." Lyn'Aya's voice was strong, calm. "You aren't alone. When we go, we'll go up to the heavens together."

Sera bit her lip. "Do you believe in an afterlife?" She never had before, but right now it sounded like the sweetest thing she could imagine.

Lyn'Aya lowered her head. "I think so," she said at last, sounding less certain than before. "Who do you want to see again?"

"Tavi. My wife."

Lyn'Aya stretched her fingers to brush the tips of Sera's. "Then I'm sure you will."

On her other side, Jas was rocking back and forth, shaking the whole pyre.

Sera glanced at her. Jas looked like she was having some kind of seizure. Her eyes were rolled back in her head and her teeth were gritted.

Mas Errol came to stand before them. "What's wrong with her?" he asked one of the guards.

"Don't know, Mas." The guard had a burning torch in his hand, holding it perilously close to the dry kindling under the pyre. This was like some bad medieval show, but there was no white knight coming.

"Doesn't matter. Probably part of the contagion."

The guard drew back, alarm on his face, and Sera breathed a sigh of relief for the momentary reprieve.

Mas Errol turned back toward the crowd. "We are here to carry out the Council's ruling, to protect the citizens of Gully-town—and this colony—from harm—"

Jas' eyes were black as pitch. "Nooooooo!" It was more a scream than a word. A dark flame erupted around her hands, darker than any normal fire, and the ropes that tied her fell away, reduced to ash that flew up into the sky on the sea breeze.

Sera gasped. The pyre was untouched by the strange flame.

Mas Errol turned to look at them and took a step backward as if he'd suffered a physical blow.

Jas' hair turned to flames too, the same dark fire wreathing her brow like a crown but not burning her skin.

She stepped away from the pyre and strode toward Mas Errol, each step seeming to take an immense effort, as if her feet were made of stone. Her hand raised accusingly. "You will not harm this one or her friends." Her voice was deep, raspy like the crunch of feet on gravel. It filled the air, silencing the crowd.

Mas Errol stumbled backward, falling back on his hands in the wet grass. "Wh… what in the gully hells are you?"

There was a strange sound behind them now too, like the rustling of the wind through a forest.

Sera turned away from Jas' strange appearance and her mouth dropped open. A strange purple wave was advancing on the crowd from the valley beyond the landing field. "What in the fucking hell is that?" she whispered to Lyn'Aya.

Jas' mother had a grim smile on her face. "The hencha are rising."

The guard holding the torch dropped it into the wet grass, where it sputtered and went out.

Jas seemed to grow even taller. She held out her arms, her long-tapered fingers pointed up to the sky as if she held the fates in the palms of her hands as the purple plants approached behind her, walking on white roots in a strange three-legged gait. "Those are my children. You call them the hencha." Her voice was growing smoother, as if whatever was speaking through her was learning how her vocal cords worked. "Bring me Mas Vellin."

The crowd parted like a wave to reveal the man, who

looked like he was desperately trying to get away. It pushed him forward and spat him out, depositing him on the ground next to Mas Errol.

The first of the hencha arrived. They were nimble things, their purple leaves rustling in agitation. As more came, they filled in the gaps, forming a wall with the pyre as its center.

Sera stared at them in wonder. They were like a purple sea, waving together without any wind, and they extended as far as Sera could see into the distance.

One of them approached her, and purple leaves wound gently around Sera's arms. Soon the rope fell away from her wrists.

She rubbed them to restore circulation. "Thank you."

One of the leaves reached up to touch her face, a gesture Sera decided to interpret as "You're welcome."

Whatever was happening, she was glad that Jas seemed to be in control of it. She took Lyn'Aya's hand and they went to stand behind Jas.

Lyn'Aya's daughter bent over Mas Vellin. "For two centuries, you have taken everything my children had to offer. You have protected them from the heyfa and for this I have been grateful." Her hand swept out to indicate the massed hencha. Somehow it looked like a branch, the gnarled wood of an ancient tree. "You have used them for food, for clothing, even to make the paper for that silly… declaration." She reached out a gnarled hand to snatch the paper Mas Errol still clutched and it burst into black flame, falling away into ash like the ropes. "You have tried to strip the wildness out of us, to tame us, to make us your slaves."

"Who are you?" Mas Vellin's face was white and beaded with sweat, but he managed to get up and stood his ground.

"I am the hencha queen. I am the sum of all of us, from root to branch, from the dimness of time through this very moment. And I say *No More!*" She slammed the butt of her staff against the ground—where had that come from?—and the whole field shook. "You will not harm this one who has been so kind to us, who alone among all of you can be a bridge between our peoples. She who was conceived among us, on the longest night."

She leaned down and stared at Mas Vellin, her gaze as hard as wood. "Do you understand me?" She reached out to put a long wooden finger under his chin, her face inches from his.

They stood that way for a moment. The whole world was frozen, save for the rustling of the hencha. The strange birds circled above, but even the breeze from the sea had stilled.

Sera held her breath. *Tavi would have loved this.* She reached out to squeeze Lyn'Aya's hand. It was ice cold.

Mas Vellin turned away first. "I understand."

"*Louder.*" Jas' voice was gravel again.

"I understand!" He pissed himself, the front of his pants darkening.

Jas straightened up and spread her arms again, glaring at the crowd, her head twisting around like a snake's. "Don't disappoint me." To the assembled horde, she said "I will send this one as my representative to your Council and together we will forge a deal that suits both of our peoples."

The flame went out and suddenly it was just Jas standing there, staring blankly at the crowd.

JAS SUCKED IN A DEEP BREATH, as if she had been drowning, and blinked. "What happened?" One moment she'd been walking toward the pyre, her stomach full of lead. And then she was standing *here*, with everyone regarding her in fear.

She looked around, taking in all the people, Mas Errol and the other man beside him with the wet pants, and strangely, the hencha plants all around them.

There'd been fire, but she was unburned...

Jas turned to find her mother and Sera standing behind her. "Mamma—"

Lyn'Aya's eyes fluttered shut and she fell to the ground.

"Mamma!" She ran to Lyn'Aya's side, kneeling next to her.

Sera sat in the grass at her mother's other side. The runner held out her hand. "Give me the DNH."

Jas pulled the black stone out of her pocket and handed it over.

The hencha closed protectively around them, rustling with agitation.

Sera took it and turned it on. She scanned Lyn'Aya's prone form with blue light, reaching out to take Jas' hand. Her hand was warm, alive.

The DNH beeped. "Severe Vitamin C deficiency indicated. Treat with supplements." The device went black.

"What does that mean?" Jas frowned.

"Your mother's not getting enough Vitamin C."

Jas looked at her blankly.

"It's a deficiency—they used to call it scurvy. Short-haul pacers get it all the time." She frowned. "Used to get it. Do you have any citrus fruits here?"

"Citrus?" Jas was unfamiliar with the word.

"Something your mother stopped eating must have supplied it."

Jas thought about it. "She only eats grains and vegetables and a few hencha berries. She *did* stop drinking her morning juice a month ago, even though they say we're supposed to."

Sera nodded. "That could be it. Don't suppose you have any?"

Jas shook her head.

One of the hencha plants sidled up, then paused as if asking permission.

Jas stared at it. *What's happening?*

Sera squeezed her hand. "Let it."

Jas reached out to it and one of its leaves touched her hand. *Tliala.*

Jas. She nodded and stood back, not sure what she was allowing. But the hencha had never wronged her. Not the way that humans had. She could trust them.

The plant knelt and put a leaf across Lyn'Aya's forehead.

"What happened to me?" Jas watched the plant as it examined her mother—one of the strangest things she had ever seen. She had the mother of all headaches, and her whole body ached.

Sera stared at her. "You really don't remember?"

Jas shook her head.

"You… channeled something. The hencha queen, it called itself. You grew taller—I know, I swear—I think you're some kind of bridge."

Vague memories were seeping back into her mind. Pressure in her head. Fire in her bones… or water? A voice like gravel. Her mother and an angel in the hencha grove. "Bridge? What the hell does *that* mean?"

"I guess we'll find out." Sera put her arm around Jas' waist and pulled her close.

Tliala straightened, and another leaf unfurled, holding out a handful of yellow berries. *Take. Help.*

Jas held them up wonderingly. She had never seen berries that color.

Take. Help. Tliala shook its leaf gently.

Jas did as she was told. The berries were warm in her hands. She knelt to give one to her mother.

The hencha plant shuffled back to its companions.

Jas put her hand on Lyn'Aya's forehead.

Her mother's eyes opened. Her skin was cold to Jas' touch.

"Here, mamma. Eat this. The hencha says it will help." She put one of the yellow berries in Lyn'Aya's mouth.

Her mother nodded and chewed the berry.

Jas squeezed Lyn'Aya's hand. Somehow she had succeeded, against all odds. If Sera was right…

"It will take a couple weeks, but she should get better. Scurvy is entirely reversible." Sera touched Jas' shoulder. "Thank you for saving me, again."

Jas laughed harshly. "I wish I could take credit, but it wasn't me." Jas wasn't sure how she felt about being a bridge. Or a puppet. *Or whatever I am.*

Sera turned to stare at the hencha. "Listen."

It was soft, subtle, but unmistakable. The hencha were singing, a sweet, ethereal tune like a hundred reed flutes. She closed her eyes. She'd heard that song before. In her dreams.

"Jas." Her mother squeezed her hand.

She kissed Lyn'Aya's forehead. "You're gonna be okay, mamma."

"Come here." Her voice was raspy.

Jas put her ear close to her mother's lips.

"When the ship came, I made a mistake. I put my angel first." Her voice was faint, her breath warm against Jas' ear. "I let them drive me off the council."

"Mamma, I won't—"

"No!" Lyn'Aya's was more forceful than Jas would have expected. "You have a chance to make things better this time. You have *power*." She turned toward Sera. "Was this truly the last Run?"

Sera nodded. "Yes, ma'am. I believe so."

Lyn'Aya nodded. "You're here for a reason, dear. Together, you two will change things in the Heartland. I can see it."

Jas met Sera's eyes. A small grin slid across Sera's face, followed by a shadow of sadness.

Tavi. Jas reached out to squeeze the runner's shoulder.

"Jas, you have power now," Lyn'Aya repeated. "Use it wisely."

Power. I have power.

"Thank you, mamma." She squeezed her mother's hand.

She felt the stirring in the back of her head again, but she wasn't scared of it anymore. *I am the hencha queen.*

Lyn'Aya brushed her away. "Now go. You have work to do."

"I can't leave you, mamma." Not after all they had been through.

"Torry will take care of me." She coughed, but her color was a little better. "He's a good boy."

As if summoned, the flitter pilot appeared through the wall of hencha. "You okay, Mim Aya?"

"I will be. Help me up and take me back to the sisters. I want to take a nap."

Jas grinned. *That* was more like the woman she knew. "Okay." Jas stood and took Sera's hand, helping her stand. "You ready?"

Sera nodded. "I have no fuck—" A glare from Lyn'Aya brought her up short. "Absolutely no idea. I think so?"

Jas kissed Torry on the cheek and pulled Sera after her. Who knew what the future would bring for her and the runner, but the future seemed bright. "Let's go change the world."

The hencha parted and they went out to meet the Council.

END

THE EMP TEST

387 AL

The Emp Test takes place in 387 AL (After Landing), a little over a hundred years after The Last Run, and thirty years before the events of the Tharassas Cycle. Again, many things have changed - Gully-town is now Gullton, for one, and a proper big city. The Highlands are now shared by steaders from the Heartland and the ce'faine, causing unavoidable tension...

TEMPEST

Lightning flashed hot across the green and gray Tharassan sky, sending Critter into a *ka-thumping* gallop through the waist-high purple trine grass toward the Redflight range to the south, erasing all the hard work that Jey'Lyhn had taken to calm it. "Slow down, Critter! He scratched the soft ridge between auracinth's bony neck ridges, but she refused to heed him.

The rain-smell was strong, sharp in the air, the bitter-sweet smell of the oils the purple, three-bladed trine grass let off that always portended rain in these high climes.

Breaking out of the grass, the headstrong aur smashed right into a tall mud *orinth* nest, shattering it into a million chunks of dirt and covering Jey with dust. Orange and green insects burst into the air in a cloud all around them, chittering their displeasure—*keeyip keeyip keeyip.*

Jey growled and flattened himself on Critter's back until they were past the swarm. He spat out dust-turned-mud and hauled back on the reins, but the aur ignored him. *Second-generation domesticated, my ass.*

Jey clamped down on his own fear and anger. He'd been stupid to take the aur out of the stable on an afternoon like this, mad or not. His anger often got the better of him. His cheek still stung where his father had backhanded him.

You will never, ever do that *under my roof again. Am I understood?* The words had stung as much as the blow. *You're betrothed, and that's the end of it. We need this alliance.* Had father told Berryl's family about the kiss? His face burned just thinking about it. There was no place in the homesteads for a *bunter.*

Jey pulled back on the reins again, but the aur seemed spooked by the howling of the wind and the heavy rumble of thunder and lightning raging all around them. Jey had been half blinded by rage and needing to be anywhere but on the Lyhn Steading, and the weather was the last thing he'd concerned himself with.

Heavy green-tinged clouds poured through the Gap, rising up from the Heartland off to the west and bearing with them the heavy moisture of the sea. The wind whipped the first drops of rain across Jey's cheeks, stinging his raw, bruised skin.

As his mother always said, *things don't always go to plan.* Jey was learning the truth of it now. "Come on, Critter." He pounded his fist on the aur's shoulder to get through its thick furry scales. "Turn around, now. That's a good beastie."

But Critter plunged on across the open plain of the Highlands with a will of its own, refusing to heed the cries of its self-appointed master. They were farther south than Jey had ever gone, getting close to cheff territory. He'd heard the savages would skin any steader alive who they happened upon unarmed. *That and worse.*

He should just jump, fall into the soft embrace of tall purple trine grass and let the creature go. Likely the aur would make it back to the ranch house of its own accord, but if it didn't, the loss would be on Jey's hands. Papa wouldn't like that.

Still, it looked to be a nasty drop from Critter's back, with the rain and the speed the aur was making across the grassy plain, and the walk home would be damned long. Jey was far afield from his usual haunts, and with the tall stands of purple grass all around, he despaired of ever finding his way back, especially without the aur's well-developed sense of *home.*

He gritted his teeth and held on.

Another sharp crack of thunder and the skies opened up as the rain poured down in earnest, soaking his back and shortening his view by a hundred paces. Still, the aur didn't slow, and the plains passed them by in a blur.

Critter was starting to smell as its fur scales soaked up the monsoon rain and its skin gave off its own putrid scent. No matter how much he washed them, the aur always gave off a rank odor when it rained. *It's nothing to what I must smell like right about now.* Jey managed a bitter laugh. He hadn't bathed in almost a week, waiting for the autumn rains to refill the Lyhn Steading catchers.

Critter stumbled, almost throwing him off, but Jey held tight with one hand on the reins and the other on one of Critter's bony ridges, his legs locked tight around the aur's barrel frame. He stared into the thickening darkness to figure out what was happening.

The aur came to an abrupt stop and tried to backpedal, but the ground slipped away beneath it. It danced on a precipice, trying to keep its footing.

Jey saw all this in flashes of light in the stormy gloom.

The yawning gap of air that had opened up before them.

The loose ground shifting under panicked hooves.

The earth giving way.

The last thing he remembered was a dull throbbing in his leg as Critter fell, shrieking like a banshee and waving its horned head in the air, into the dark chasm below.

AVAIN WHISTLED one of the work-tunes his mother had taught him as he hauled the red-headed steader's body into his cavern, pulling him gently off the travois he'd constructed to carry the poor man. He eased Red—his name for the stranger —onto his own bed, a soft palette made of trine grass and an aur's inner hide. Then he reaffixed the outer hide to the edges of the small cavern's entrance to keep out the worst of the storm.

Avain put more dry wood on the fire near the mouth of the cave. Then he set about brewing some of the hencha tea his mother had taught him to make, and her mother before her, and so on back to the time of the *passage*, when his ancestors had followed Mas Cha'Fah away from the restrictive culture of the Heartland in search of something better, passing through the Gap to find the purple plains of the Highlands.

Avain said silent thanks for this gift from the hencha queen, which he had gathered from the four directions— North, South, East and West. Hencha here grew wild in small stands, always in circles to defend against the invasive heyfa weeds that would suck the life out of the purple plants. His mother had told him about the vast fields of hencha in the Heartland, swaying and singing their alien song.

Red groaned, twitching. His broken leg was swollen and blue. Avain had done his best to set it when he'd found the steader trapped under his aur in the gully. Now that Avain had hauled the man out of the storm, he'd brace Red's leg so it could heal properly. The steader was his enemy. *Still, I can't just let him die.*

He'd go out the next day to skin the aur and save its hide.

Avain's emp stirred in its skin pouch behind his ear, picking up something from the steader, who was still knocked out. *Pain. Fear.*

It's okay, little one. He'll be better soon. The stranger was an adult, if just barely. About the same age as Avain. *Maybe he's going through his own Aud'ling.* Avain's self-enforced distance from his tribe for his testing hadn't been easy, especially the first few weeks.

Leaving the tea to brew, he took a softened piece of aur hide and dipped it into the cool water in a reed basket. He wiped the stranger's brow gently, letting the cloth linger on his raised cheekbones, willing the coolness into the steader's body to chase out the spirits of heat that possessed it.

He ran the rag over Red's chest. *What's your real name?*

The man's eyes flickered open and went wide. "What in Heaven's Reach?" He looked around wildly, but Avain put a hand to the man's lips. The steader tried to sit up, but then dropped onto the makeshift bed, lines of pain etched his face.

Avain patted Red's shoulder, feeling for him. The man must be in excruciating pain.

He checked the fire again, stirring the coals and whistling another of his mother's songs, a mournful one that fit the mood of the day. The wind blew in a scattering of leaves from outside, and they skittered across the floor like little inthyms. He pulled the hide covering back and glanced up at the gathering clouds—the storm had spent its fury, but there would be rain again by morning.

Avain brought back the small earthenware cup of the bitter hencha tea he'd brewed. The fellin root would help with the pain.

He eased the steader up. He held the cup to Red's lips and mimed *drink.*

The steader scowled. "What is it?"

Avain wished he were allowed to speak. It would make this all *so* much easier. He mimed *drink* again.

Red glared at him, but he took a hesitant sip. "Ppthhh." He spat it out, sticking his tongue out in distaste.

Avain held the cup to the Steader's lips again, daring Red to defy him.

The steader grunted but tried again, managing to swallow a few gulps.

When the contents of the cup were gone, Avain set it next to the fire. He laid Red back down. Their eyes met, and Avain felt like he was being studied. Judged.

What's your name? Why are you here?

The steader's eyes gave him no answers.

Avain passed his hands over Red's face, pulling the lids gently shut. The steader sank back into sleep without further urging.

Through his emp, Avain could feel the steader's relief as the tea worked its magic and the pain slipped away. *The fever is passing.* It was a good sign. *In the morning, his head will be clear.*

Satisfied, he pulled the blanket up over the man's shoulder, and settled in with his back to the cavern wall. He would eat something, see what he could do about the man's leg, and then try to get a little sleep himself.

It was good to have some company—he'd always hated being alone.

STRANGER

J ey tossed in his sleep, dreaming fitfully about the storm, rain falling hard as hail all around. The wind was whipping through his hair, and he felt the ground slipping out from under him once again…

He awoke with a start. Instead of a downpour, a soft but steady rain fell outside, soothing in its *pitter-patter*. The pain in his leg had lessened. Jey opened his eyes. *Where the hell am I?*

Firelight flickered across the rough cavern ceiling, creating strange twisting shadows, and someone was whistling a melancholy tune.

He stared at the rocky ceiling above him for a minute, trying to make sense of things. His head still ached, and his thoughts were as slow as hencha sap. *This isn't home.*

He turned his head to see the stranger regarding him curiously from across the room. The man's skin was a deep, beautiful tan, sunbaked like his own from harsh hours under the Highlands sun. Cheff for sure—the swirls of ink on his cheeks were proof enough of that. His face brought back a rush of memories—huddled over him, the cool touch of cloth on his burning skin, the taste of the bitter drink he'd almost spat out. Well, he had spat out some of it. He *did* feel marginally better.

"Sorry. I'm not feeling like myself." He winced again as the leg pained him. His hand reached down to touch the collection of cloth and sticks that encircled it. *Must be broken.* He took a deep breath to keep himself calm. *You know what they do to an aur when it breaks a leg...* His brother Col's voice was as clear as if he were right there next to him.

Jey wondered what had happened to Critter. He feared the worst.

He looked over at his host again. "Who are you?"

The cheff stared at him.

Jey felt anger stirring again and repressed it. He was lucky he hadn't been skinned. Yet. He looked around the room, seeing all the things the man had stored there. Was this his home? Father had told him the cheff lived in caves like savages.

There were several green and gold skins stacked on the far side of the cavern, next to a little fire—mountain ix, probably. Jey was impressed. Those critters were hard to catch, the way they could climb an almost vertical surface.

An assortment of earthenware jugs and canisters in one corner by the fire might hold just about anything, as could the aur-skin pouch that hung from a stick on the wall. By the dim light coming in through the edges of the narrow cavern entrance, it was some time in the morning—a gray and stormy one.

"Well, whoever you are... I'm glad you found me." *Catch more inthyms with sugar...* He shifted, wincing as pain shot up his leg.

The man picked up a stone knife, stood and advanced toward him, his eyes fixed on Jey's. Jey tried to scramble backward. *This is it!* He couldn't go far with a broken leg and the rock wall behind him. Fear and anger warred inside him. He'd never been very good at controlling his emotions.

The man knelt before him, running his thumb along the flat side of the knife.

Jey closed his eyes, waiting for the knife to plunge into his throat. Instead, he heard a scraping sound. His eyes flickered open, and he saw the man finish writing something into the dust by his straw bed. He stared at the man, who gestured toward the word.

Jey leaned over to read it in the dim light, still wary of the sharp knife. "Avain," he read aloud.

The man tapped his own chest.

"Your name."

The man nodded.

"You… can't speak?"

Avain tilted his head.

"You won't speak."

A nod.

"All right."

Steaders and cheff rarely interacted, despite sharing the Heartland, and when they did, it was often bloody. Being *rescued* by one? That was something new.

"I'm Jey," he managed lamely. How did you act normally after almost wetting your breeches in front of someone?

Avain nodded. He gestured toward the sleeping palette and put his hands next to his face, miming sleep.

"Sleep? Yeah. Sure." Jey *was* exhausted. "You're not going to hurt me, are you?"

Avain shook his head with a snort.

I should get up. Go home. Something.

Avain mimed sleep again.

Yes, mas. Only partly reassured, Jey lay down and closed his eyes. Sleep claimed him quickly, worn out as he was by the simple exchange.

It occurred to him as he drifted off that he was probably sleeping on Avain's bed.

THOUGH HE'D VIOLATED his oath of solitude by bringing the steader to his cave, Avain didn't have a choice. Jey would've died without his help. Though surely his mother wouldn't see things that way. "Cheffah help cheffah, and he's not one of us," she'd say, sending a wave of disapproval from her emp to his. The Steaders were still Heartlanders, though they'd come to the Highlands a generation before.

But then again, his mother hadn't seen Jey laying helpless in the gully, leg crushed by the weight of his aur. Avain couldn't have left the man there, steader or not.

The swelling in Jey's leg had gone down, and the setting brace he'd constructed from carved auley sticks looked good. Avain felt a surge of satisfaction at his own work. With the will of the gods and some luck, Jey might walk on it again with little trouble. Though he'd always feel the spirits of the weather, like Avain's aunt Ellya, who'd broken an arm as a girl.

Jey was watching him now, eyes glinting in the firelight as Avain cooked the grains that would make a warm morning meal. He could feel the man's gaze on his back, almost as warm as the fire itself, but he gave no outward sign of it. Jey was frightened enough to find himself in the company of a threatening stranger—Avain could feel the fear coming off of him in waves. And he was itching to be up and around.

Avain turned and flashed what he hoped was a non-threatening smile.

"Morning." Jey gave him a half grin in return, and his eyes lit on the carved wooden bowl in Avain's hands. "Or is it afternoon yet?"

Avain didn't reply. He set down the bowl and helped Jey get propped up against the wall. The man winced, but only slightly. *A good sign.* The muscles of his arms were tight, corded like hardwood.

He handed Jey the bowl.

The steader needed no urging. He used his fingers to scoop up the warm cereal and shoveled it into his mouth, as if he hadn't eaten in a month.

Avain laughed. *Hungry this morning.*

Jey just looked at him quizzically.

For an answer, Avain retreated to the back of the little cavern, and pulled out a woven basket filled with dried *hacka* berries he'd picked up in the mountains the week before. Bringing them back with him, he sat beside Jey, and began to feed them both from the basket, savoring their sweet, salty flavor.

The man mumbled his gratitude. There was an undercurrent of… something. Embarrassment? Shame?

Avain just nodded, unsure how to respond. He leaned forward to wipe off Jey's forehead, their cheeks close. His smell was clean, strong, and his emp sensed a whiff of desire.

Avain's eyebrow went up. He pulled back and they stared at each other, noses inches apart.

A spark passed between them, but then Jey turned away. Avain felt a wave of shame from the steader. He was confused—what did the steader have to be ashamed about? He pulled back, giving Jey some space.

After a moment, Jey looked at him again, and reached up and touched the raised spot behind Avain's left ear where his emp lived. It twitched a little at the steader's touch.

Jey jerked his hand back, his eyes going wide, radiating disgust and fear. "What the hell?"

Avain frowned. *I'm sorry.* Whatever the reason, Jey was spooked. By the emp? The crackling energy between the two of them? Avain's face flushed at the thought of having frightened his guest.

Maybe the steaders didn't have emps.

Avain turned away and gathered his hunting gear—the short bow his father had helped him make, the hunting knife painstakingly crafted from mountain shale under the watchful eye of his mother, and the hide sack that he used to haul back his kills.

With a last apologetic glance at Jey, he fled, feeling the steader's eyes still on him.

PAIN

ey watched Avain go, his mind reeling. *What in Heaven's Reach was that?*

His face flushed, and his whole body was hot, racing along with his mind on this new tangent.

Jey's heart *thrummed* like he'd just run ten kilometers. *What's happening to me?* Only Berryl had ever made him feel like that. *And what the farking hell was that thing behind his ear?*

He tried to get up, but a searing pain shot through his leg. He sank back down onto the pallet, tears squeezing from the corners of his eyes, growling with frustration. *I will not cry.* He hated being stuck here like a fenced aur.

Jey slammed his hand into the pallet, sending dried grass flying everywhere. Then he reached out and grabbed one of Avain's earthenware jars and threw it against the wall with all his might. It shattered, raining hencha berries and shards of pottery across the cavern.

But his anger hadn't run its course. He grasped the hide across the cavern entrance and pulled at it. The rough skin resisted him, so he found one of Avain's stone knives and slashed it again and again, putting pressure on his broken leg in the process.

So much anger. So much pain. Stuffed down inside for years. Hiding how he felt, who he was, what he wanted. What he needed. *Something has to give.*

The pain of it—both physical and emotional—finally broke through the dam inside him, and it all came flooding out.

Jey lay there in the morning sun, grasping the furry scales of the torn hide tightly in both hands. He didn't care about the stench.

He stared at the bleak sky and the long stretch of empty hills before him, not a clue where he was or how to get back home.

He began to cry, sobbing in ragged gasps and forlorn moans, wringing himself out like a wet rag until there were no more tears left inside him.

~

AVAIN MADE his way across the grassy highlands to where he'd found Jey, running through the tall purple grass, wary of predators. Dead beasts often attracted flocks of jexyn, hive birds that were dangerous after they had a taste of fresh meat. And though they were rare, eircats sometimes prowled the grasses, searching for prey late in the summertime when mountain hunting was scarce.

Jey must have been riding the aur when it fell—he'd had spurs on the back of his boots, and there were deep, triple-toed prints at the edge of the ravine.

He smelled the remains of the carcass before he found it. It was washed up on a rocky shore a few hundred meters from where it had fallen, rotting under the purple sun. Scavengers had been at it, and there were triple-grooved eircat-tooth marks on the bones. *Not much to salvage.* Jey would miss his mount.

Avain spent the next few hours hunting, bagging a few skerits to use for dinner.

He returned to the cavern as the sun was about halfway through the green bowl of the Highlands sky. The autumn storm season was here, bringing almost daily sooners, storms that swept out of a clear green sky in the early afternoon to drop rain on the summer-parched land. By dusk they were gone, leaving behind a clear, crisp night. The rains had been plentiful thus far. The cheffah would eat well through the winter.

There were clouds pouring through the Gap even now, and with luck there'd be rain before the sun had crossed another quarter of the sky. Avain could smell it coming as the sweet oils of the trine grass filled the air, the harbinger of Highlands rain. The grass rustled, untwining its three purple stems and folding unto a cup, ready to capture the precious drops of water.

Avain raised his eyebrow as he approached the cavern entrance. The hide that protected them from the wind was… different. It had been torn, and then sewn back together with some trine grass cord from Avain's stores.

Some pottery shards were scattered across the hillside below.

He hoped nothing had attacked the cavern while he was gone, and that Jey was unharmed.

Avain pulled back the hide to find the steader sitting up against the cavern wall, looking healthy enough. His eyes fixed on Avain's neck for a moment, and then he looked away. "I made us something to eat." Jey gestured to the fire.

Avain felt a flash of guilt from the steader. He glanced at the fire, noting one of his jars was missing. He bit his tongue but said nothing. He knew the signs of a fit of anger. He'd thrown them often enough himself, before the emp. But Jey was a grown man—Avain was surprised he'd never been taught to control himself better.

A clay pot hung over the fire, filled with water from the waterskin and assorted herbs and dried meats. All of this activity must have pained Jey, but the steader smiled as he watched Avain take it in.

Avain felt the man's guilt melt away.

"Soup." Jey gestured for him to try some.

Avain knelt and dipped his finger into the mixture. It was warm and thick. He brought his finger to his mouth and tasted the so-called soup.

He suppressed a grimace at the saltiness of it but managed a smile for the man before he turned away to take a quick gulp from his waterskin. The cool water washed the taste away. *Must be feeling better.*

He knelt to examine the man's leg. It was still swollen, though the color was better.

Jey winced as Avain touched the purple skin. "Owww!"

Pain. Avain's emp writhed around a little and then settled. Avain grimaced, flashing him a quick *sorry.*

Jey watched his neck, but said nothing.

Avain set about preparing a poultice to put on the leg, and some more of the pain-relieving tea, aware that Jey's eyes followed his every move.

Soon he had the man sleeping again, and he set about his own afternoon devotions. The wind set the hide to flapping back and forth as the rain began again outside the cave.

They had reached a détente, but like the calm before the storm, it couldn't last.

THE EMP

The next week passed quickly. Avain and Jey fell into a pattern together—each morning Avain would rise early, stirring the coals and adding more wood to the fire.

Jey would try to catch a glimpse of whatever that thing was on Avain's neck. Usually the emp was still, but sometimes the skin pouch would rise and fall, or twitch like there was something alive under Jey's skin. It was the creepiest thing Jey had ever seen.

Maybe Avain was *infected*. Highlands fever? Though he'd never seen a fever blister so large. Or one that *moved on its own*.

Jey would look away and watch the smoke rise from the improvised fireplace. It should have filled the cavern, but instead it disappeared somewhere high above, through the rocks.

He chafed under the restrictions imposed by his injury. His parents would be missing him, and his father would be furious at his absence. Each day, he grew more irritated, struggling to keep his anger in check.

Sometimes he lashed out at Avain, especially when the

cheff was poking at his leg. He regretted it instantly, but Avain seemed to take it in stride. The man would grab his hunting gear and go out past the hide that kept the wind and cold out, vanishing for hours while Jey looked for ways to keep himself occupied.

He hadn't washed in days… or was it weeks? He could smell himself, and he longed for a fresh mountain spring where he could wash away the worst of the grime. With his broken leg, though, he wasn't going anywhere, anytime soon.

Avain would eventually return, and Jey would talk while the cheff man listened, nodding.

Jey spoke about his life on the homestead, about his family and the livestock they raised to sell in the Heartland. Sometimes he talked about the day of the fall, though he carefully edited out the reason he'd left the Lyhn Steading. During these sessions his anger would slowly dissipate as the words poured out of him.

He wondered why Avain remained silent. *Why won't you talk with me?* Cheff were people, just like homesteaders. They even shared a common tongue. But Avain wouldn't speak a single word of it, at least not while they were together.

Avain didn't try to get close to him again. If that's even what had happened. Jey was no longer sure. There had been *something*. A lingering moment between them that had been charged with electricity.

Jey felt a growing connection between them, one whose nature he was hard-pressed to describe. Still, it was there, along with the stirrings of his body and heart.

As the days passed, soon he was able to hobble about on his injured leg, though it still pained him. He sometimes made his way to the cave mouth to watch Avain leave on his daily outings and would wait there, like a lizard basking in the warmth of the sun, for the cheff's return. His anger burned low, banked like the hot coals of the fireplace.

The autumn storms continued without any particular

pattern. As they became soaked in rain, the Highlands began to bloom with orange and purple huercinths and pezzywinkles, always in matched pairs.

One morning, Jey sat on his perch at the cavern's entrance, watching a pack of inthyms making their way through the hardscrabble below the cave mouth, hunting for food. One would pop its white head up above the rocks, peering around for predators, its ears swiveling. Then it would emit a sharp whistle, and the troop would emerge from various hidey-holes and run across the rocks to their next redoubt.

Jey saw the stirrings of life all around him, things he'd never bothered to notice before. A cherry fly the size of his thumb landed at the edge of the cavern, watching him with its glossy eyes, one of its twelve black legs idly scratching its round red abdomen. Above, a *skerit* spread its leathery wings and rode a warm vortex of air up into the sky.

The break was healing nicely. Soon he'd be able to make his way back home to the homestead. To Mother and Father. Back to mending fences and tending livestock. *They must be worried sick about me.*

His anger flared, but he pushed it down again. *I don't want to go back.* He wished he could stay here, with Avain, in a Highlands cavern forever. What kind of future did he have, youngest son of a big family, suitable only to be married off for the family's benefit?

Maybe he could take Avain back with him and have Mas Ausey take a look at that weird thing on his neck. He snorted at the absurdity of that thought. *Not likely.* They'd run the cheff off the homestead, or worse.

After a couple hours, Avain returned, grinning as he climbed the hillside toward the cavern. He carried a couple skerits, their thin gray bodies hanging limply from his belt. He skinned and roasted the little creatures on a spit, and he and Jey shared a meal together.

Jey felt better when Avain was around. The anger receded,

and he was able to breathe again. Soon, though, this all had to end.

He tried not to let panic overtake him at the thought.

~

As the days grew steadily shorter, Avain felt a companionship growing between them. He wasn't sure what Jey was to him, exactly, but he was something more than just a steader.

Through his emp, Avain could feel Jey's slow-simmering anger, especially when he first returned from his hunting trips. Anger at being trapped here, no doubt. At feeling like a caged animal.

He could do something about that, something to help Jey feel human again.

He put some water on the fire to heat up and pulled out a bit of reed soap he'd brought with him from home. Most days he just bathed himself in the canyon, not too worried about his own smell. But Jey would have difficulty making the trip, and surely he was sick of smelling himself after being cooped up in the cave for weeks.

Jey watched him intently, his eyes following every move. Avain mimed cleaning and handed the soap over to him.

Jey smelled it, and a grin broke out on his face. "Soap!"

Relief flooded Avain's senses. Avain nodded, setting the now-warm water next to Jey's grass bed. He handed the steader a washcloth made from the soft inner hide of an aur, motioning him to clean himself.

Then he went outside, giving the steader some privacy.

There was silence, then a bit of splashing. The sharp minty smell of reed soap emanated from the cavern.

"Avain?"

He poked his head inside.

Jey sat there, naked, holding out the soap and washcloth. "Wash my back?"

Avain nodded, his face hot. A strange mix of feelings emanated from Jey—shame, fear, desire.

Avain sat behind Jey and soaped up the cloth. He ran it down Jey's back while he whistled a song his mother used to sing to him in the bath.

The steader shivered.

Avain rang out the dirty cloth over the pot and washed Jey's naked back again until it was clean. His skin there was startlingly white, though the tan on his arms and legs was fading fast too.

"Thank you." Jey turned to stare at him. Their eyes met. Avain was intensely aware of the steader's nakedness.

Jey raised his hand toward Avain's neck.

The little emp conveyed only strong *interest* to Avain. No fear this time. Avain took Jey's hand and guided it to touch the emp's skin-pouch. *It's okay, little one. He won't hurt you.* With Jey's hand, Avain massaged the pouch gently to coax the creature out.

Slowly it poked its head out. It was tiny… maybe as long as his pinkie finger. Its big brown eyes squinted in the relatively bright light, and its ears twisted to find Jey.

Jey whistled. "What is it?"

Avain sighed. He'd already broken one rule of his testing. He was no longer *alone*. And there was no way to explain an emp to Jey through a series of grunts and scribbled gestures. "It's an emp."

Jey looked up at him, his eyes going wide again. "You *can* speak."

Avain cleared his throat. It felt strange to talk again. "I'm not supposed to. I'm being tested." Though it was a personal test more than a formal one. Only he'd have to live with the knowledge that he'd failed some of its strictures. "Hold out your palm."

Jey frowned, and *doubt* flashed through Avain's head. "It won't bite me, will it?"

"No, it won't hurt you."

Jey held his hand open. *Trepidation* was overlaid with *trust.*

The emp crawled from its pouch, its pink three-toed feet touching Jey's skin as if testing the water. Then, satisfied, it slipped out in one smooth motion and curled up on Jey's open palm, emitting a soft purr.

"It's… beautiful." Jey lifted it to stare at it more closely. "Can I touch it?"

"Yes. Like this." Avain mimed running his finger lightly over the little form.

Jey copied him, and the purr increased, as its furry body rippled between gray and warm brown.

"It likes you."

Jey flashed him a bright smile. "What does he do?" He handed the little emp back to Avain.

Avain held it up so it could slip back into its home.

"It helps me sense what other people are feeling. Helps us harness our own emotions too, and to regulate our reactions." He closed his eyes, remembering his mother's face when she had given him his first one when he was fifteen.

"Can you read my mind?" *Alarm* radiated from Jey's mind.

Avain shook his head. "No. Only feelings."

Jey relaxed a little, but some of the *distrust* was back. "Doesn't it feel… weird to have the… emp? Inside of you?"

"Oh they aren't inside. They make a pouch on my neck, grown from my own skin." The look Jey gave him made him laugh. Avain managed a wry grin. "I guess they *are* inside me. Just a little."

Jey nodded, but Avain could tell he was still taking it all in. "Want to grab a few of the yellow hencha berries? I'll get dinner started." He turned his back on the steader, letting Jey have a little privacy to process his thoughts.

Avain was used to his emp. All of the highlanders got them when they came of age. But it had to seem very strange to Jey.

SHARED WARMTH

Jey's eyes flickered open, and he edged himself up onto his elbows to look around the cavern. Sometime after he'd fallen asleep the fire had died down to embers, which provided the only light in the enclosed space. On the far side of the small cavern Avain was fast asleep, snoring softly, his back turned to Jey.

He wondered if the little emp slept too.

That had been a revelation. They said the hencha queen could ride a human, but this was different. To feel what everyone else around you was feeling? How could that not be disabling? Maybe that was why Avain lived out here alone.

Still, he wished he could feel what Avain was feeling now. To know if he was alone in his longing.

Jey lifted the fur off his legs, wincing at the twinge of pain that traveled up his shin. The old fur was smelly, redolent of dirt and oil and mild decay, but it was warm.

Trying to move as quietly as he could through the dark space, he managed to reach the entrance without waking his sleeping companion. He pushed his way through the hide that covered it, legs first, moving awkwardly on his butt.

Outside, the night was black as pitch.

Jey leaned against the cool stone of the cliffside and took a deep breath of the cold air. It came out in a fog. His eyes slowly adjusted, and soon he could make out the stars, including the spiral of the Serpent's Tail glowing a gentle green overhead.

Somewhere below was his father's steading, the patch of land granted to him by the government back in Gullton, for him to farm as he saw fit.

Somewhere there, too, was Bes'Ela's home, another steading not far from his own. They were promised, matched by their parents, and one day soon they would marry, sealing the alliance between the two farms.

He couldn't do it. Not now. Something had shifted inside of him. Or maybe opened up. Something that had started with Berryl, and that kiss.

Not her fault. Bes was a good person. She didn't deserve to be married to a bunter like him.

He couldn't go home. Not now. *I don't even know how far away it is.*

Here he was, spending his days and nights with one of the cheff. Whenever Avain touched him to check his wounds, shock waves ran up Jey's body, and not from pain. Had Avain cast a spell on him? *Could they do that?*

The pain in his leg had subsided to a dull ache, and it did look much better, though he couldn't see it very well in the dark. Jey reached down to touch the skin between the braces. It was still rough in places, and surely still the greenish-purple color it had been the day before. But it was healing.

He felt restless. Trapped here in this cavern, unable to take care of himself. Stuck between what he had been and what he was becoming, though he had no name for it. His anger rose again, and he pushed it back down ruthlessly.

A cold breeze blew up from the highlands, and he shivered. It was freezing out—autumn was slowly giving way to winter.

He pushed his way back into the cavern and moved to stir the embers like Avain had shown him. Then he set a couple more logs on the fire—wood that Avain had cut to keep them warm.

He reached his hand halfway across the distance between them, wanting to touch the cheff, softly, to feel the smoothness of his skin.

Avain shifted in his sleep, turning over onto his back.

Jey jerked his hand back, cursing at himself under his breath. *What is wrong with me? What would Father think? What about Bes?* He couldn't go back. He couldn't stay here. Not forever.

There was no answer from the surrounding walls, only the soft, warm light from the fireplace embers to calm his shivering form.

He climbed back under the furs and closed his eyes, but it was a long time before he finally went to sleep.

AVAIN WOKE UP. *Something's wrong.* He could feel it in his bones, like the touch of the ancestors. The emp stirred in his pouch, feeding off the steader's own troubled energy.

The rain had cooled the heat of the day before, and now that the clouds had fled, the night was all the colder. Avain sat up, looking over at his guest. Even though the furs covered him, Jey lay shivering in his sleep.

He crept over to Jey's side and pulled a rough loom-woven blanket up over his shoulders, on top of the furs, to warm him. The steader still shivered. Avain's hand on his forehead confirmed what he'd feared. Jey shivered—his body wasn't accustomed to the cold outdoor temperatures in the late fall and early winter.

His brother would have called the steader weak, but Avain knew Jey was anything but—he just had the chills.

Carefully he settled himself over Jey's shivering body, taking care not to jostle the man's injured leg. Then Avain lowered himself, putting his arms around Jey to warm him.

At first the shivering seemed to get worse, and Avain could hear the man's teeth chatter. *Nervous energy* came through the emp. He set his cheek against Jey's, and at last he could feel the steader's emotions settling. Avain closed his eyes, remembering long warm nights snuggled next to Kavin, skin to skin, just like this, their emotions running in synch through their emps.

Kavin had never returned from his testing.

Soon Avain's Aud'ling would end, and he would need to return to his own people. Jey had to be well enough by then to take care of himself.

Even in sleep, Jey's anger was there, bubbling just below the surface like the mud pits of Anghar Mor. There had been no further eruptions since the hide-tearing rampage, but it was only a matter of time.

Avain needed to do something about Jey's bottled-up anger. He knew, then, what he had to do.

He closed his eyes, willing himself to go back to sleep, but the idea persisted in his mind.

He sighed. It was too late to do anything tonight. There would be time enough to see to it in the morning.

After another hour, he finally fell into a deep sleep, blissfully unaware of anything else until first light.

THE TEST

Jey watched Avain hungrily, as the cheff prepared something for them to drink by the fire. The hot, bitter tea did not taste nearly as bad as it had on that first night. He had slowly grown used to it over the intervening weeks, and it did help with the pain.

The swelling of his leg was almost gone, and he could touch the skin now without wincing. It looked like Avain had set it clean; he would walk normally again, before long. He knew they didn't have much time left together. When he could walk, he could go home. That thought only made Jey feel bitter.

He remembered the touch of Avain's cheek against his the night before, the warmth of the other man's body next to his. He'd given up trying to rationalize it, to understand these feelings that were coursing through him. All he wanted was to hold Avain next to him, to feel the warmth of that golden-brown skin against his. And that scared Jey like nothing else.

Avain returned to Jey's side with two cups of tea. Jey took his gladly, letting his hand brush softly against Avain's in the process. The nervousness settled a little as he sipped the bitter brew and it trickled down to warm his stomach. When he'd finished the whole thing, he set the cup aside and took Avain's hand.

The man looked up, his eyes filled with a knowledge and understanding far older than his years. Next to his gaze, the memory of Bes's face seemed pale, unreal. Avain reached up to the skin-pouch where the emp lived and coaxed it out into his open palm. The little creature looked around, blinking, its ears swiveling around. Its eyes came to rest on Jey's.

Jey no longer felt a sense of revulsion. Instead his mind filled with calm.

Avain pointed at the emp and then at Jey's neck, a question on his face.

Back to silence, are we? Then he realized what Avain was asking. "One of those… for me? I… no, I don't think so." He wasn't *that* used to it. "Besides, it's yours. I couldn't…" Still, a part of him wondered what it would be like to *feel* someone else's emotions.

Avain grinned.

Bastard. "You *felt* that, didn't you?"

Avain shook his head, holding up the emp. "Of course. You can't while he's out of his pouch. You… I'm just that obvious?"

That smile again.

Avain held his palm flat and ran a finger gently up and down the emp's little gray form. Its eyes closed, and it shivered, emitting a soft purr.

Jey watched, entranced. The little creature's vibrations increased, and soon it was just a gray blur in Avain's palm. "What's it doing?"

Avain pointed at his eyes, and then back to the emp.

"Watch. Got it."

Suddenly the vibrations stopped, and Jey blinked. There were now two emps, each smaller than the original. "Holy Highlands… was that like… emp sex?"

Avain grinned. He gently picked up one of the emps with

his other hand and let it slip back into its little pouch. Then he offered the other to Jey.

Jey frowned. *I don't want this. Do I?* No one back home would understand it. *He* didn't even understand it. And yet… the emp exuded a palpable sense of peace, of calm. Of… love? Or something farking close.

Jey's father wasn't there. Neither was Bes'Ela. Only Avain. Sometimes life took you somewhere you never expected until you got there. He swallowed, hard. "Yes. I'll do it." He felt a rush of adrenaline, the hair on his arms standing up.

"One more thing."

Jey looked up into Avain's eyes. "Speaking again?"

"For this… I must. In the bonding, you'll face your greatest fear. The thing that keeps you awake at night."

"I have no fear."

Avain chuckled. "I didn't think I did either."

Jey frowned. *What am I afraid of?* "Will it… hurt me?" He shivered.

"Yes. But it can't kill you. Not if you give in to it and accept it."

Jey nodded. "Sounds easy." The dark look Avain shot him told him otherwise. "What was yours?"

Avain was silent for a long moment. "I'll tell you after," he said softly. "Ready?"

Jey searched his eyes. "Yes. I trust you." And it was true. Damned if he knew why, but there it was.

Avain reached up to hold the little creature next to Jey's neck. Jey felt it questing over the tender skin there, and then it slipped off of Avain's palm and settled itself.

Jey searched Avain's eyes. "Is that it? I thought there'd be—"

His world collapsed into darkness.

~

GENTLY AVAIN LAY Jey back down on the rough bed. The steader's skin felt hot, and beads of sweat pooled on his forehead, running down his face in little rivulets.

Avain retrieved some water from the wooden bowl outside that had collected it from the last storm. It was cool and clean. He took a soft cloth and dipped it into the water and then wiped Jey's forehead.

Avian's own bonding was still vivid in his memory.

A RUSH OF COLORS. Avain felt sounds, tastes and emotions blended together in a cacophony of sensation. He tasted purple, heard a yellow hencha berry's distinctive flavor in his ears. Remembered the sound of the pain in his arm when he'd broken it as a child. All jumbled in his head.

Then eerie silence. His mother had tried to prepare him for this.

The sensations slipped away, leaving nothing but raw, primal fear.

He was all alone. Left behind by his people when they migrated to a new home. He woke up in the middle of a dark cavern, with only a blanket and his clothes.

Fear seized him as the darkness closed in on him like a flock of jexyn. He threw off his blankets and raced through the cave, calling out "Mamma, mamma!" like a cub child.

There was no one. His piteous cries echoed through the hollow, bleak cavern as the fear seeped into his veins like ice, freezing him in place like stone.

AVAIN SIGHED. He'd received his emp a long time ago, but that trial had shaped his current testing. It was why had to live here alone. To face his demons.

Jey's eyelids fluttered, his skin clammy and his breathing shallow.

He faced his own test now.

~

JEY'S HEART RACED, his emotions taking on form and color and tearing at him like a wild animal, exposing his heart and guts. He pushed his way through an earthen tunnel, roots and claws reaching for him, each inflicting its own taste, sound, scent, image or feel on his naked self. Then he was back home in the stables, lying on a pile of hay, pants down to his ankles.

Berryl'Ela, Bes's handsome brother, was on his knees between Jey's legs, the afternoon sun dappling his back. Big, beautiful, strong Berryl. There'd been much more than a kiss, this time. Jey was in a state of bliss, finally doing what he'd longed to do for so long.

A shadow fell across them. Jey looked up, fear seizing his chest.

His father scowled at him, disgust etched in every line of his face. "Jey… you… what the green holy hell?"

Berryl stopped what he'd been doing and looked up, his face going whiter than an inthym's hide. "Mas Erris. I… I…"

"Get the hell off my steading, Mas Ela. I'll talk to your father about this later."

"Yes sir." Berryl gathered his clothing and scampered out of the barn, past Jey's sister who had just come around past the door.

"Eeeew. You and Berryl?"

"Enna, go into the house." Father's voice was ice.

"But papa…"

"Go!"

Jey had never heard the man so angry. His face was hencha-berry-red, and he clenched his hands into fists at his side. His father advanced on him, and Jey scrambled backward, desperately looking for his clothes. His father grabbed him by the scruff of his neck and dragged him out of the barn, scraping Jey's knees. He pulled a coil of rope off the barn door on the way.

Jey cried out, but a stern look silenced him.

He threw Jey up against one of the sturdy fence posts. "You want to be naked in the barn? You can be naked out here instead." Then he threw the rope around him, pulling it so tight that it bit into Jey's ribs.

Jey held back his tears as some of the other steaders gathered around to see his shame.

When his father had finished his handywork, he stood back to take a look at his trussed-up son.

Jey tried to shift his hands to cover his nakedness. He closed his eyes, not wanting to look at his battered knees, or at his father.

"This young man has violated the rules of the steading. He has spilled his seed with another man, not with a woman as is right and proper and necessary for the growth of the community. Although he is my son, he shall suffer the same penalty as anyone else who commits a crime—a week on the post with only bread and water."

"No, papa..." Jey looked into his father's eyes at last and was silenced by the disgust reflected there.

"We are not *cheff* up in the mountains with no rules, no laws, no morals. We live by the Charter." His father spit on him. "After one week, you will be freed, and we will never speak of this again. *Ever.* Do you understand?"

Jey closed his eyes. "Yes, papa," he whispered.

"Louder, boy." His father nudged him with the toe of his boot.

"Yes, papa!"

Unsaid was what would happen to him if he ever broke the rule again. "Good boy." Like he was five years old. His father turned to go.

Jey's anger returned then, rising up from his gut and

filling him like a volcanic eruption. His stomach twisted, and his vision blurred. "No," he muttered.

His father stopped. He turned, his face curled into a snarl. "What was that, boy?"

Jey didn't care. He glared at his father, and the fire from his eyes was reflected in his father's gaze. "I said *no*." Jey straightened up, his skin burning. He *was* on fire, but the flames didn't hurt him. The rope burned away from him, and he stood, no longer embarrassed by his nakedness.

His father took a startled step backward.

"I will no longer bow to you or do what you say." Each word came out with the force of a bolt. "I'm not a child. No longer *your* child." Electricity raced up his spine, and he felt *alive*.

The other steaders slipped away in the darkness, but his father was immobilized, transfixed by his stare.

He took a menacing step forward, thrilling to his newfound freedom. His father had no power over him anymore.

Only then did Jey realize it. His father was afraid. *He's afraid of me.* The man's legs were shaking, and a wet patch appeared on his trousers.

Jey's anger collapsed all at once. All this time he had been afraid of his father, of the way the man bellowed and ordered him around. And all this time, his father had been afraid of *him*.

The flames went out.

His father's face faded from view, and Jey collapsed, again wracked by sobs. This time he cried for his lost childhood. For his old self. For the days when life had seemed simpler. And for his father's fear and anger.

Ever so slowly, his rage leaked out of him, evaporating into the cavern's darkness like smoke, leaving him shattered and empty.

AFTERMATH

Avain heard Jey's long, drawn out sobs and ducked back into the cavern. The steader had thrown off the covers, his skin beaded with sweat. The emp snuggled against his neck, its new pouch beginning to grow up around it, thin and translucent.

Avain took a soft aur-hide cloth and dipped it into the bowl of cool water. He wiped Jey's forehead, letting the cool rivulets run down the other man's face to dampen the straw below.

Jey's eyes flickered open, but he stared blankly at the ceiling. Avain hovered above him, looking into his eyes. There was nothing there. The testing had been rough.

Some of the tested came through it damaged, broken by what they'd learned about themselves. One of Avain's cousins, Havir, had hidden away from the sun for a year before he finally ventured back into the open. He'd never told Avain what he had seen, but he still feared bright light.

Avain leaned back to get more water. Jey's arm grabbed his, hauling him back.

Jey's eyes focused. His voice came out dry and raspy, as if he'd been screaming. "What… did… you… do to me?"

He spoke rather than gestured, "Here, drink this." Avain picked up an earthenware cup, which he had prepared with heartroot, fellin, and a pinch of peat while Jey had been dreaming.

"What…"

"It'll help you sleep. No more dreams." Avain held the cup up to Jey's mouth, lifting his head to help him drink the milky mixture.

Jey's lips twisted in distaste. "It's awful."

Avain grinned. "Helps with the voice too. Drink it all."

"Yes, papa." Jey grimaced again, from the taste or something else.

"Good. You're going to sleep for a day. Relax."

"Sounds… good." Jey's eyes drifted shut. Avain?" Jey's emp shifted in its pouch.

"Yes?"

"Thank you." His hand reached out to touch Avain's face. Then he was out.

Avain sat watching his guest, though Jey was more than a guest now. He was the first steader to receive an emp.

Avain pulled the hides over Jey's naked form. His temperature should return to normal soon—he'd be cold if he wasn't covered up.

Avain stood, sparing one last glance at Jey's sleeping form. Then he slipped out of the cavern to check his traps. The steader would be powerfully hungry.

JEY SMELLED SOMETHING DELICIOUS. His eyes flickered open. Avain was turning the spit over the fire. It held an umvit, if he guessed right, its three wings stripped of their dark purple, scaly feathers, their tips singed by the fire. Fatty juices dropped onto the flames, sending them upward in sizzling greed toward the cooking meat.

He lay there, letting the dream roll through him. His father. The flames. The anger and shame he'd been holding inside all these years.

Jey reached up and touched the little pouch on his neck. His emp turned over, sending him warmth and satisfaction. Colors exploded in his head—red and blue and purple where they overlapped.

"Feeling better?" Avain didn't turn.

"Yes." The colors twisted to become *satisfaction* and… something else. *Regret*? "What was in that stuff you gave me… hey, you're talking again!"

Avain nodded. "Yesterday was the end of my testing."

Jey swallowed. Hard. "Did you pass, or fail?"

Avain shrugged. "I *survived*. The rest will be decided later." Again *regret*. Definitely regret.

Jey frowned. He pressed on, happy to have someone to talk to again. "Decided by *who*?"

Avain only grunted. He was *annoyed* with all of Jey's questions. Jey could feel it. Like a knot at the base of Avain's skull, squeezing tighter every time Jey asked another question. Annoyed was green, tinged with red. Jey reached up again to touch the pouch where the emp lived next to his own skin. It shifted and *purred*, and Jey felt a wave of contentment.

"Here." Avain had carved off a chunk of the umvit's breast and put it in a bowl along with some cooked grains.

Jey sat up, wrapping the hides around him to preserve some dignity. His stomach rumbled. He took the meal and ate greedily—it was delicious, but there was a strange tang to it. He and his brothers had gone umvit hunting before, using bolos weighted with smooth river rocks to bring the ungainly creatures down from the sky after one of them flushed them out of the tall grasses.

The image of his father looming over him flashed through his head—arms on hips, a scowl slashed across his face as if carved by a knife. He took a deep breath.

"What did you see?" Avain was sitting in front of him cross-legged, staring at him intently.

Jey blushed. "I… my father. He found me. With another man."

"And…?" Avain looked puzzled.

"It's not allowed. We have to breed. To fill up the valley."

"Why?"

That stopped Jey cold. "Because… if we don't, there might not be enough of us."

"For what?" Avain had stopped chewing to stare at him.

"To keep growing."

Avain raised an eyebrow. "Why do you need to keep growing?"

Jey laughed, chagrinned. He'd never been asked that before. Why did they need to breed? To take over the world? And then what? Father always said that the steaders had left the Heartland so they could do what they wanted. Somehow, though, that didn't apply to him. "I don't know."

Avain laughed, a full-throated sound that Jey had never heard from him before.

Jey felt his delight and looked up, surprised. The emotion was bright and yellow in Jey's mind. "What?"

"We have that in common, at least." He finished his bowl. "Want more?"

"Yes, please." Jey was starving. He handed the bowl back to Avain sheepishly.

Avain squinted at him. "Your anger is gone."

Jey closed his eyes. Avain was right. He felt… lighter. That tight knot between his shoulder blades had loosened its grip. "You're right." He looked into Avain's eyes. "What did you see? What was your fear?"

Avain shoveled more of the grains into the bowl, then carved off another hunk of the dark purple meat. He handed it over, and Jey accepted it gratefully. "I was alone."

Jey stared at him. "That's it?"

Avain cracked a rueful smile. "I've been afraid of being left alone since I was a boy."

Jey had grown up surrounded by family, by ranch hands and aur and all manner of other farm animals. Sometimes all he wanted was to be by himself. "Different cultures."

Avain nodded.

"So… if your time here is over…"

"I'll leave for home within a few days." He took both bowls and rinsed them out, spilling the waste water outside the tent through the hide flap.

"You're going to leave me?" Fear seized his heart. *Maybe I'm afraid of being alone too.*

Avain stiffened. "You're healed. You can make your way home. To your own kind." He radiated *regret* now as he stripped the meat off the umvit with ruthless efficiency, putting it into a larger pot already filled with water. He added the grains and carcass and set it to cook above the fire.

Jey looked away. It was strange to be so connected to Avain's every feeling, but it was comforting too. They couldn't hide things from one another.

He didn't want to think about losing Avain. Not after all that had happened between them. He tested his leg, stretching it outside of his hide coverings. It looked pale, but the pain was gone, the wound shrunk to a red scar. "I guess I'll be okay." He could feel tension in Avain's mind. There was *fear* now too, and *resignation.*

And *desire.* Scarlet desire.

It matched Jey's own.

Jey reached out to put his hand on Avain's cheek. Gently he drew Avain's face toward his and brushed his lips against the cheff's. Avain's were warm and soft.

Avain's desire flared, stoking Jey's own. Then it was just as quickly banked, fading to nothing.

Jey's emp stirred, moving about as if uncomfortable.

Avain pulled away, his eyes downcast

Jey stared at him, trying to pierce his feelings. How did Avain feel? Did he truly long for Jey the way Jey longed for him?

What was stopping him?

"I shouldn't. It's… I'll be gone soon."

"I don't want to think about tomorrow." Jey had waited so long for this. He wasn't about to let Avain get away now.

"You sure?" The man looked up at him, his eyes unreadable, but the desire had returned. Emps didn't lie.

Jey nodded. Outside, the rain started to fall, softly at first, then harder, a pattering drumroll that soon blocked out all other sound from the world beyond the cavern. They were all alone together, in this perfect place at this perfect moment.

Avain's lips quirked up in a slight smile, and his desire clear in Jey's mind.

Jey drew Avain down with him in the firelight, and this time the cheff responded with an ardor to match his own.

Jey felt safe, connected, electric as he began to explore Avain's body, his tongue tasting the cheff's salty masculinity, feeling his firm muscles go taut under his beautiful skin.

For a few moments they fell through time together, and Jey finally let go of his fears, his doubts, and his shame as their bodies entwined.

The fire slowly flickered down to embers, but neither one cared.

DECISIONS

The next morning, Jey was alone.

He got up on his still-unsteady legs and made his way to the cave mouth. Avain was nowhere to be seen.

Jey sat there, watching the rain cascade across the highlands in wide curtains as the trine grass drank it in. And like spears tossed by the gods, the lightning raced from the sky to earth. The thunder rumbled ominously closer, but still he did not move.

By nightfall, Avain had not yet returned, and the rain forced him back inside the cavern.

Jey was surprised how much he'd come to depend on the man. Avain had opened up to him in a way he'd never expected. The men on the steading weren't *allowed* to have feelings. At least, not feelings that weren't sharp and jagged.

He touched the emp's pouch behind his ear, his fingers brushing it lightly, and felt a surge of warmth and appreciation. His understanding of the cheff was clearly, woefully inaccurate. The steaders viewed them as savages, but if his experiences with Avain were any guide, he had much more to learn.

Maybe Avain was gone for good, and Jey had missed his chance to make him more than a short acquaintance.

Jey sighed. Resigned, he left his post at last, and set about making something for the two of them to eat, memories of the night before flashing through his mind.

If Avain returned.

If not… it made him heartsick to consider it.

AVAIN WAITED until late that night to re-enter the cavern, when he felt Jey's sleeping contentment. He gathered his belongings with the stealth of an eircat, not wanting to awaken Jey. He spied the bowl of cooked grains and dried meat Jey had left out for him and smiled.

He would miss the steader. They'd shared something the night before, a joining that would never be repeated. They were from two different worlds. There was no place for either in the other's life.

Silently, he left out enough supplies and water in a basket to get Jey through another week or two. He had his own people to go back to. Still, he wished that he could spend a few more days with Jey.

It was the night of the new moon, when he was to return to his mother's hearth and become a man. No longer did he fear being alone.

He left one more gift for the man, perched atop the stores of wrapped meats and grain.

He lingered a moment more, watching Jey's sleeping form. "I'll always remember you," he whispered. Then he was gone, a ghost into the cool fall night.

Jey awoke to the first light of the new morning, and stretched, pulling the ache out of his muscles. He looked around the cavern expectantly, and then sat up in alarm. Avain's things were gone, except for a few bundles left at Jey's bedside. He jumped up and ran to the cavern entrance, already feeling much steadier than a few days before.

"Avain." There was no answer. "Avain!"

He'll come back. Maybe he's only gone out to check his traps. But Jey knew that the man had left him for good.

Jey lay back on the pallet and wept, knowing he was acting like a child, not like the hard man his Father wanted him to be. Not like his brother Col.

He didn't care. He cried for the loss of a friend who'd somehow been more than a friend. For the possibilities he'd tasted and been denied. For someone Jey never really knew.

At last, no more tears would come.

He didn't know how long he had lain there, only that the sun was nearing its zenith in the green sky when he returned to himself. He sat up slowly, groggy from the sleep and tears, and used some of the water Avain had left behind to rinse his face and hands. It was only then that he saw the other gift Avain had left him.

He picked up the aur-hide cloth and opened it. It was a little doll, made of dried reeds, in the form of a miniature aur. Jey smiled, then laughed out loud at the toy. Somehow Avain had known about Critter.

Jey had a choice. He could accept his destined fate, returning home to tell his family about his adventure, to show them the wondrous emp. Though he wasn't sure they would understand even a carefully edited version of events. To marry Bes, if she'd still have him.

Or he could go after Avain. He'd learned enough from their late-night conversations to find the man's cheff tribe, and Avain had left him everything he'd need to try.

Jey stood and shouldered the basket, tied the water-skin

to his waist, and left the cavern one last time. The autumn rains were gone, and the green sky was cloudless and clear.

As he shuffled away from the cavern mouth, he was a different man than the inexperienced youth who'd fallen off his aur a few weeks before.

He took a deep breath of the fresh late-morning air, staring down the valley toward Lake Zeraya. He had a whole life down there. A steading. A family. A woman to whom he was betrothed. His father's ranch couldn't be too far away.

It seemed like a different man's life.

The emp stirred next to his neck. What had once disgusted him now filled him with hope, with the possibility of a life he'd never known he could lead.

All it takes is a first step.

He turned away from the valley, heading up into the mountains without looking back, whistling one of Avain's cheerful tunes. *I'm coming.*

Love this book? Keep on reading - you'll find book one of The Tharassas Cycle, The Dragon Eater, here with all the buy links:

Get it Here

ABOUT THE AUTHOR

Scott lives with his husband of 25 years in a leafy Sacramento, California suburb, in a little yellow house with a brick fireplace and a couple pink flamingoes out front. He has always inhabited the space between the *here and now* and the *what could be*. Indoctrinated into fantasy and sci fi by his mother at the tender age of nine, he devoured her library. But as he grew up and read the golden age classics and more modern works as well, he began to wonder where all the people like him were.

After he came out at twenty three, he decided that it was time to create the kinds of stories he couldn't find at Waldenbooks. If there weren't many gay characters in his favorite genres, he would reimagine them himself, populating them with a diverse universe of characters. He would subvert them and remake them to his own ends. And if he was lucky enough, someone else would want to read the things he wrote.

His friends say Scott's brain works a little differently – he sees relationships between things that others miss, and gets more done in a day than most folks manage in a week. Although he was born an introvert, he learned to reach outside himself and connect with others like him.

Scott writes stories that subvert expectations, that seek to transform traditional sci fi, fantasy, and contemporary worlds into something new and unexpected. He also runs both Queer Sci Fi and QueeRomance Ink with his husband Mark, sites that bring people like them together to promote and celebrate fiction that reflects their own reality.

His writing, whether romance or genre fiction (or a little bit of both) brings a queer energy to his stories, infusing them with love, beauty and power and making them soar. He imagines a world that *could be*, and in the process, maybe changes the world *that is*, just a little.

He was recognized as one of the top new gay authors in the 2017 Rainbow Awards, and his debut novel "Skythane" received two awards and an honorable mention.

He runs Queer Sci Fi, QueeRomance Ink, and Other Worlds Ink with Mark, and is the committee chair for the Indie Authors Committee at the Science Fiction and Fantasy Writers of America (SFWA).

ALSO BY J. SCOTT COATSWORTH

Liminal Sky: Ariadne Cycle

The Stark Divide | The Rising Tide | The Shoreless Sea

Liminal Sky: Redemption Cycle

Dropnauts

Liminal Sky: Oberon Cycle

Skythane | Lander | Ithani

Liminal Sky: Tharassas Cycle

The Dragon Eater | The Gauntlet Runner (Sept 2023) | The Hencha Queen (Mar 2024) | The Death Bringer (Sept 2024)

Other Sci Fi/Fantasy

The Autumn Lands | Cailleadhama | Firedrake | The Great North | Homecoming | The Last Run | Wonderland

Short Story Collections

Spells & Stardust Collection | Tangents & Tachyons | Androids & Aliens

Contemporary/Magical Realism

Between the Lines | I Only Want to Be With You | Flames | The River City Chronicles | Slow Thaw

99¢ Shorts

Translation

Audiobooks

Cailleadhama | The Autumn Lands | The River City Chronicles | Skythane (Feb 2023)